the Great Cat CAPER

Lauraine Snelling

Kathleen Damp Wright

the S.A.V.E. Squad

BARBOUR
PUBLISHING

D1016871

Published by Barbour Publishing, Inc., P.O. Box 719, Uhrichsville, Ohio
44683, www.barbourbooks.com.

*Our mission is to publish and distribute inspirational products offering exceptional
value and biblical encouragement to the masses.*

Member of the
Evangelical Christian
Publishers Association

Printed in the United States of America.
Dickinson Press, Inc., Grand Rapids, MI 49512; August 2012; D10003469

Dedication

Kathleen—
to my husband, Fred, my Adventure Guy

Lauraine—
*to Chelley and Gina of Have a Heart Humane Society in my
hometown who have saved the lives of hundreds of cats and kittens.
My hat is off to animal rescuers of all kinds.*

Acknowledgments

Kathleen—
Thanks to: Rhonda at Second Chance for Homeless Pets in
Salt Lake for letting me experience the joy of cat-ness and ask
a jillion questions. The Wang family for whisker instruction.
Jane Owen, a fabulous friend and writer who laughed in all the
right places and marked up some that needed to be better. Mom
Kris and daughter Gaby for how accelerated school might work.
Natalie for use of her made-up word. No More Homeless Pets of
Utah for letting me see the process of trapping community cats.
Lauraine for her friendship and our continuing adventures.

Lauraine and Kathleen—
God, You are our Treasure in every moment.

Chapter 1

Beetle!

*A*nd now I want you all to sit somewhere *unstructured* and think of your own interjection." The language arts teacher waved her arm, draped in gauzy fabric, and smiled, showing most of her teeth. Vee Nguyen's slow, answering grin flowed across her face; the woman winked at her. "Put the brains that got you into this accelerated learning center to work!"

Vee, pleased to be noticed, blushed and looked down. Yes, she and these kids were smarter than the rest of them. She couldn't wait to tell her new S.A.V.E. Squad friends, Sunny, Aneta, and Esther, that Moby Perkins Elementary School Accelerated Learning Center—or the ALC—was like another planet. The girls—the first letter of each name spelled out "S.A.V.E."—had agreed to meet at the library today to tell each other *everything* about the first day of school.

To beat the others, she darted toward the rolltop desk where Mr. Tuttle, the learning center teacher, sat. Rather than the students leaving the center, teachers came into their learning center. Mr. Tuttle said it was to continue the "synergy" of learning. Vee had made a note in her always-present notebook to look up the word. She crawled under the desk. With the next breath came visions of her twin stepbrothers, the Twin Terrors. Where she sat smelled just like their feet. Only extra-strength grown-up stinky. Eww.

No matter.

From her prime spot, she watched the rush for the padded window seats, the couch, and a huge white claw-foot tub loaded with rainbow-colored pillows. The room burst with brightly colored kites hanging from the ceiling and words applied to the wall: WHO WILL YOU BE TODAY? PREPARE. PROPEL. PERPETUATE. The good spots were going fast. Giggles and a couple of grumpy "Hey, I was here first!" floated in the sun-brightened air.

Better get going with A+ work. This was her spot, this group of smart kids. She'd earned it. *What interjection would be better than everyone else's?* Breathing through her mouth like she did when she was around the Twin Terrors, she readied her pen. She grinned, keeping her lips nearly closed, placing her hands on the carpet to get a smidge more comfortable. How cool to make up your own word for—

"Eww!" she shrieked and shot out from under the desk. The heel of her left hand had *crunched something*.

The language arts teacher clapped her hands. "Excellent learning moment here, Vee!" She turned to the class who was—yes. Staring. At. Her. Vee's face burned with embarrassment. Staring at her after she had the best interjection was okay. But now? No way! The teacher turned back to Vee, looking expectant. "What interjection to show strong feeling or emotion could you use for this intensity, Vee?"

Dreading what she might find, but needing to know, she slanted a glance down at the "whatever" now stuck to her hand. What interjection? *Think, Vee, think.* This is life in the ALC. Parts of a beetle, antenna still moving on a separated head, lay there.

"Beetle!" she yelled, madly shaking her hand. "Beeeeeetle!"

Nodding to the class to join, the teacher clapped. "*Beetle* works. Strong consonant beginning conveys strong feeling."

Oh—Vee fished around for a better word to describe her humiliation. Okay, *beetle*. As she stood there feeling like a *beetling* idiot, the class went back to their papers, most crossing out what they had.

"You've done a great job," the woman said. "Go ahead and continue the rest of the activity."

Yanking her focus from the remains of the bug, Vee plunged in. The loud and smelly stepbrothers could have each other and soccer mania. Her parents and their others could have each other. She had *her* spot.

If I survived the beetle incident and fish sticks with marinated vegetables for school lunch, I can survive anything. Now, back in the smart-kid learning center for fifth period math, a tiny, yes, *tiniest* zizzle buzzed in her stomach along with lunch. The feeling couldn't be because math was the next class, she argued with herself. She'd worked hard all summer on her math. It had to be lunch. She wrote in the notebook:

Bring lunch except for pizza day.

"Okay, nodkins." Mr. Tuttle folded massive arms across an equally massive chest. "Get out your books. Stay awake in class." He knit bushy brows. "Ms. Smith and math begins in a minute, and before she does"—Mr. Tuttle looked at the generic wall clock and then down at his clipboard—"I'll tell you about your service-learning project for the semester." When he smiled, he looked like a wolf baring its teeth like in Wolf Week on the *Everything Animal* show. Her gaze fell to his large, clog-covered feet. *Eww.*

A hand touched her shoulder. She jumped. Looking up to her left, she saw the guidance counselor. The woman smiled, looking over Vee's head in Mr. Tuttle's direction with a little tip of the head toward the door. *I am once again the center of attention the first day of school.* Sigh. Mr. Tuttle kept talking as though the counselor wasn't there and everyone wasn't staring at Vee. "Service-learning projects help you see that just because you may be the smartest kids in the school, every-thing is not about you. . . ."

After they sat down at a small round table in her office, the petite guidance counselor picked up a polka-dotted file folder with Vee's name on the tab. The counselor opened it and laid it flat on the table between them.

"Oh, Vee. First thing, you're not in trouble," she said, as though she'd forgotten any kid would freak when dragged off to the counselor's office the first day of school.

"I know," Vee said. Although she *had* wondered. "I'm not a troublemaker. I'm one of the smart kids."

"You are," the woman nodded. "Here's the situation. We had a com-puter glitch after all the students took the assessment to get into the Accelerated Learning Center."

The zizzle swept up from Vee's toes. She found she was still clutching the notebook and pen. She set them both down on her lap and unclenched her fingers.

"The thing is," the counselor said slowly, leaning forward and looking right into Vee's dark brown eyes. Her gaze was kind, which let

Vee know something terrible was up. "You passed the assessments in language arts, history, and science."

Vee counted one, two, three subjects. The counselor hadn't mentioned. . . "But, not in—" Vee faltered, her voice sounding breathy like her *okay, no problem* voice when Dad called to say he wasn't coming to pick her up like he promised. "Math?"

The counselor shook her head. "Not in math. It will take me a day to get everything arranged. You can stay in the ALC until then," the counselor said, patting Vee on the shoulder and smiling. "Don't think of it as losing something. Think of it as blooming in a different place."

Blooming? How could she bloom with her prized spot yanked out from under her?

This time the list formed in her head:

Why Smart Kids Cry the First Day of School

Her throat tightened. After school. The Squad. They were going to tell each other everything.

Everything?
No way.

Chapter 2

Upset Plans

There it was, Oakton Community Center. Vee bounced to rearrange the weight of her backpack. Before today it was a good place—where she met the girls who were now her best friends. She sighed. "I just can't tell them what happened at school today."

A squirrel ran in front of her and up a tree, chattering. "I don't care what you would do," she said to it. "I'll just have to think of something." The bushy-tailed rodent flicked his tail in response and dashed out of sight into the upper boughs.

"Sure." Vee brushed her black-as-night bangs out of her eyes. "Desert me when it gets a little tough." There was no putting it off. Vee's stride grew longer and longer until she was running, backpack digging into her back with each bounce. She'd probably get cuts in her back that would get infected. She would die. Math will have killed her.

Regular sixth grade tomorrow. Not what she'd worked so hard for. As she stopped and put her hands on her knees to catch a breath, she looked up. All she had to do was turn the corner. The girls would be waiting on the library steps.

From behind her, she heard running feet. Two little girls, wearing school uniforms like the ones her friend Aneta wore to school, pounded past.

"I'm telling Mom first."

"No you're not. I was the one who was chosen, not you."

"You get everything first. I'm telling Mom—"

"Yeah, like it's all about you. You only talk about yourself. . . ." Their voices faded out of earshot.

Plan:

1. *Get the girls to tell all about their day.*
2. *Before Esther asks. . .*
3. *Check Anti-Trouble Phone and shriek, "I have to get home!"*
4. *Go home and talk to Mom and make a list to stay in the ALC.*

"It'll be stellar." This cheered her a bit after the dismal day, and she increased her speed. The library steps were empty. *Not a problem,* she thought, unloading the pack and sitting on the steps. She had a plan:

> *Tell Mom*
> *Regular sixth grade is NOT AN OPTION*

In the next breath, she heard the Squad giggles and conversation before the girls rounded the corner of the community center.

"You're kidding," Sunny's happy voice bubbled first. Of course. Redheaded Sunny's hazel eyes were always sparkling about something. She was the coolest homeschooled kid Vee had ever met. "Melissa isn't at your school this year?"

What? Scrambling to her feet, Vee pulled on her backpack. That was stupendous news! Melissa Dayton-Snipp had made Aneta's life miserable at the Cunningham Preparatory Academy where the two attended.

Blond, blue-eyed Aneta, voice always quiet, her English getting better and better, said, "No! She is living in Europe and going to a horse school."

The next voice was Esther's nasal, high-pitched voice. This time she wasn't complaining. If there was a Squadder whom Vee still had to get used to, it was the dark blond, chunky Esther. Somehow she and her narrowed, hazel stink eye tied Vee's nerves in knots. *She likes correcting me too much.*

"Yeah, I was sitting right there when the computer teacher pointed to me and said, 'Esther Martin. You must be the coordinator of the computer room for your grade!'"

Vee paused.

"Can you believe the complete yay-ness of it?" It was Sunny again. "I've been shooting pics with the digital camera my uncle Dave sent me a couple of weeks ago. My pictures got me in"—a Sunny squeal and Vee could picture her friend spinning around, arms out—"an advanced digital photography course. I'm the only kid in there!"

Three perfect first days of school. Everybody had their spot. Vee turned and fled.

Chapter 3

Prickly Lettuce,
Prickly People

Now what am I going to do? Vee had covered the distance across the parking lot before she knew what her long legs were doing. *Home. Just. Get. Home.* She pushed off with her right foot to make a sharp left turn and cut through the back of the community center. A few streets to cross, another left turn, and she'd be home. Mom would help her make a plan and this, well, *beetling* day could be over.

In another second, she saw C. P. heading toward her, looking at the candy bar in his hand. She veered off course toward the Dumpster in the corner of the parking lot tucked in an untended bunch of trees and bushes just beginning to show a turn of leaf color. Five cats, crouched on the lid of the Dumpster, scattered. Too late, she noted the rotting pear on the ground. Her left foot hit the goo, slid, and she did a split into the bushes, dragging her right knee across the pavement. As her backpack thudded between her shoulders, the wind oooff'd out of her. Face-plant. Right into a bush. Prickly lettuce, a weird weed she'd learned about in earth science last year. *Ouch.*

Three facts about prickly lettuce:
1. *You don't want it in your salad.*
2. *It grows just about anywhere in any soil.*
3. *It hurts when you face-plant into it.*

Pulling the rest of her through the bushes, she lay there for a moment, panting. Had C. P. seen her? If he had, her life was over. C. P. was way too curious about *everything*. She held her breath, listening. If he had seen her, she'd hear him pounding toward her on the parking lot cement. She closed her eyes, waiting to hear his scratchy voice. "Hey, whatcha doing down there, Vee? Looking for treasure?" Then he would laugh his hyena laugh. At that point, unbelievably, her day would get worse.

But C. P. didn't come. After her heart began pounding in her ears and she knew she'd either have to breathe or pass out, she chose breathing. *If* C. P. was coming. She sucked in a gasping breath.

No C. P.

Safe in a secret spot, behind the protection of the spiny bushes, she curled up her limbs for a few moments like a fawn then awkwardly pulled herself to a crouched position. She peered out. The Dumpster obscured most of the parking lot, but she had a good view of the library steps where C. P. had joined the S.A.V.E. Squadders.

They had to go home sometime. She would wait. The cottonwood tree's rough bark scraped against her spine. She'd learned about that tree last year, too. Moments passed. A stinging sensation began on her right knee and both heels of her hands. An inspection revealed a rash of angry, red, seeping dots of blood. Ick. More than bugs, she didn't like to see her own blood. She would probably be okay with bugs if it hadn't been for the addition of the Twin Terrors to her life.

She fumbled to get her backpack off then froze. The tiniest sound of a breaking branch reached her ear. She whirled. C. P.? She scanned the green-yellow prickly bush behind the tree, near the Dumpster. The five cats had returned to the top of the Dumpster and were sunning themselves.

Someone *was* watching her.

The softest something brushed her. Holding her breath, she closed her eyes. *Please don't let it be something like a caterpillar with creepy antennas and eighty zillion feet.* She imagined it creeping nearer to the tender, scratched elbow. Or the shredded knee. Maybe it was a rat. *Please, not a rat.* A rabid raccoon? That mouthy squirrel?

The softness spread further over her elbow. The stinging got worse. Then a rough—tongue?

Tongue?

Vee opened her eyes and forced herself to look down at her right elbow.

A bitsy scrap of a kitten was licking the blood off her elbow, squeaking as it did so. It was about two handfuls of gray kitten with black stripes and a black nose smudge. Bugged out eyes and slit-like pupils let her know they had surprised each other. Each kitten ear had a tuft of bedhead-like fur sticking straight up. Vee removed her arm. The kitten hissed and leaped backward, straight-legged.

"Shoo!" Vee whispered. Where was its mother? It was too little to be by itself. Was one of those Dumpster cats its mother?

The kitten studied her from a safer distance. Vee's right leg was going to sleep, and she moved it. The kitten showed its teeth and hissed—a tiny bit of fur with huge white fangs. Vee snorted. Tough wasn't going to work for this kitten. Then she thought of those fangs sinking into her ankle that was within biting range of the little feline. It could happen.

A heavily accented voice cut into Vee's concentration. The moment she took her gaze off the kitten, it pounced nearer.

"Go away," Vee whispered. The kitten arched its back and twitched its tail. Vee's eyes crinkled into slits, and she smothered a giggle.

A harsh voice broke in. "What good are kots vit disease and no homes? The Helpful City Festival is in almost one month. They vill not vant to see kots vit no home like this." All the V-sounding words made Vee dizzy. Crab-crawling a bit forward, Vee leaned to the left and saw a tall, spare man talking to a woman. Where had she seen her before? Medium height, silvery hair. She could be a million old ladies. She stood holding an aluminum pie pan. The Dumpster cats were watching from the lid, tails lashing.

The curious kitten darted forward and bumped Vee's hand then bounced away, back humped.

"Hey, I didn't tell you to come to me," Vee muttered to the kitten, trying to listen to the two people argue.

The woman—Vee knew she'd seen her up close before, but where? —straightened. "We started the problem. Idiots won't spay and neuter their pets. Dump them when it's not convenient anymore. They don't necessarily have disease, Hermann. Someone must save the kitties."

He interrupted. "No point to feeding the kots. Animal Control gonna get rid of them before the festival in about a month. The judges don't vant to see kots in a city that's supposed to help people."

"Hermann, you ninny. Helpful means helpful wherever there's a need. This parking lot is their home. These cats need a place."

Place. That cat-feeding woman now had Vee's attention. How could a Dumpster surrounded by ouchy prickly lettuce be an acceptable place to live?

"Der crazy in der head, Gladys. Nobody vants to help cats vit don't belong to nobody."

"If you think Animal Control is going to haul off these cats, you better think again. Not while I'm alive." The woman's voice was fierce. Hermann grumbled under his breath.

Once again a smooth softness flowed across Vee. She absently pushed away the kitten. For such a young kitten without its mother, it seemed pretty brave. She glanced down. The kitten sat about three feet away, eyeballing a fluffy caterpillar waving its antenna, marching its creepy bazillion feet halfway across Vee's hand.

For the second time that day, she shrieked, "Beetle!" and, with her backpack banging off one arm, leaped to her feet, then staggered through the prickly lettuce and into the parking lot. To her left, Hermann and Gladys stepped out from behind the Dumpster.

"What is the matter vit you?" the man snapped. "What are you doing in these bushes?" Did he think Vee had *on purpose* skidded on a slimy pear, face-planted into prickly lettuce, and had a creepy caterpillar crawl over her hand? She shuddered, scratching her hand vigorously.

The Cat Woman glared. "Are you trying to haul off my cats?" She turned a withering glance on Hermann. "Are you making children do your dirty work these days?"

Time to exit. Flinging her head up, trying to ignore the man and woman and march off with dignity, she got as far as the head fling. The S.A.V.E. Squad and C. P. stood on the library steps, their mouths hanging open.

Out of the corner of her eye, the curious kitten and the other cats shot past her, across the parking lot, loping left toward the lake. The curious kitten hopped to a stop, looked back, and made eye contact with Vee. Then it was gone. Vee felt curiously disappointed. Oh, the *beetling* day that wouldn't end!

Esther's voice sounded across the parking lot, high, loud, and accusing. Vee only heard bits. Hands on hips, "—never told us!" Esther said, ignoring that Vee had just emerged bloody, limping, and getting yelled at by two senior citizens.

Tell her what? Vee continued her painful approach. Her face ramped up sharper stings, and she gingerly patted the scratches. "I—I was tying my shoes, and a caterpillar ran over my hand." Wow. That was feeble—a word on the language arts vocab list.

"Why were you tying your shoes in the bushes?" Esther asked, fists still firmly planted on her pudgy hips.

Vee sighed. In a last effort to get at least some part of her plan in action, she yanked the ATP from her pocket and gasped, "I've got to get home before I get in trouble."

Aneta flipped her long blond hair over one shoulder and hunched her shoulders. Easily the tallest of the four girls—and everyone was taller than C. P.—she stood like she was proud of being tall. "But we did not tell about our first day of school like we said. And C. P. . . ."

Already edging away from the group, every scratched part of her in full sting, Vee wanted to know, *Why has nobody asked why my face is bleeding? Or my hands? Or why I have a full-blown bloody shred across my knee?*

Sunny spun in a circle. "Oh yeah. The C. P. thing *is* crazy. Who would have thought that?"

C. P. swiveled his head from Vee to Sunny. "Hey," he said, swallowing something. "Why would it be so crazy that I would transfer into Moby Perkins' smart kids' class?"

Vee stopped backing away. *Zizzle!* In her damaged condition, she thought her hearing must be going.

Esther stepped forward, peered, and then gasped. "You're bleeding!"

Just. Get. Home. That's all she wanted to do. Anything to get home to her mother who could begin to make some sense of the world's worst first day of school. It would be even better if it were Mom and Dad together to help her. But that wasn't going to happen. Not with Bill at Mom's house and Heather at Dad's. As in Bill and Heather, their new *spouses*.

"What is it with you and bugs?" C. P. had finished the caramel or whatever and was picking up his backpack. "First the beetle in school today and now—"

"How did you know about the beetle?" The words shot out.

Sunny led Vee over to the steps and prodded her shoulder. "Sit down. You look like you got in a fight with a cat."

"How did you know about the cat?" She sat. It had been watching her. Rather than creepy, it was—special.

C. P. wandered off. The girls clustered around Vee. She looked over her shoulder. Hermann walked down the parking lot to the senior citizen door and entered.

"Who's the grouchy guy?" Esther asked, plopping down next to Vee. With the next question, she had already forgotten him. "How come you didn't tell us C. P. was going to be in your accelerated class at school?"

Beetle.

Chapter 4

The Not-Dad and the Big Stuff

$\mathcal{B}$ill turned from the kitchen sink, holding two gigantic sopping potatoes in his paw-like hands.

"Hi," Vee said, standing in the doorway, her wounds pulsing "ow" with each heartbeat. "Where's Mom?"

Bill was a diesel mechanic, so his hands were much rougher than Dad's. Dad shook hands a lot at the business meetings he had with people who gave him money to build all his businesses. "Your mom called. It's you and me tonight for dinner. She's showing a house she thinks they might make an offer on." His dark brows went up as his wide mouth made a crazy expression. "Here's hoping, huh?"

Vee forced a smile.

> *Number One Hope of Realtors: They might make an offer.*
> *Number One Reality: They hardly ever did when you thought they would.*

"Yeah." She cleared her throat. "I'm, uh, going to do my homework."

Again the eyebrows shot toward the dark, curly hair that fell over his deeply tanned forehead. "On the first day of school?"

"Oh." She bit her lip. Her prickly lettuce rash—or this *beetling* day—was pushing her to cry.

"Anything you want to talk about—like how was your first day and why do you look like you've been in a fight?"

It wasn't that she didn't like Bill. He was just. . .*not* her father. *Her* father was taking the Twin Terrors to their soccer games and buying them tokens at Pizza Crazy. The last Dad Weekend, she'd had to go to *two* soccer games, hold coats, and cut up oranges. The Twin Terrors and their stinky feet had made her glad to return to Bill's quiet house.

Bill was trying hard to be whatever he was supposed to be in this new family blend. Trouble was, it was *aawwwk*ward. Was he supposed to be a dad replacement? Maybe he wasn't supposed to be like a dad at all. She sometimes mixed up the conversations her parents and their new-ish spouses had had with her. *"I'm not trying to replace your—insert 'mother' or 'father' here—I just want you to be part of our new life."*

> *Five Names for the Stepdad:*
> 1. *Replacement Dad*
> 2. *Next-Dad*
> 3. *Not-Dad*
> 4. *Mom's Special Friend*
> 5. *Bill*

Another sigh. Who had what spot in the family was just so. . .*weird* these days. A spot in the Accelerated Learning Center was the only safe thing. Oops. Bill was looking at her. Had she been standing there with her mouth puckered up like a baby about to cry? Her backpack slid off her shoulder, bouncing on her knee with the lettuce rash. "Ow. No thanks. It was—just school. You know."

"Not much I don't. I dropped out before I graduated." He gestured with the dripping potatoes. "I'm better with my hands working on the big rigs." He grinned the all-out smile that her mom said made her stomach wobble. *TMI, Mom.* "I washed my hands after work. You're safe."

As she headed for the stairs, Bill's deep voice followed behind her. "Your mom says potatoes take about an hour and a half for these big ones. After that we're on our own for what to put on them."

She called back, "Okay," and slogged down the hall to her room. After placing her backpack in the oversized chocolate-colored beanbag in the corner by the window, she pulled off the long-sleeved peasant blouse that had been way too hot for the first day of school and pulled a T-shirt over her head. Grimacing, she peeled the capris off her bloody knee. Those pants would take some explaining to Mom. After pulling on shorts—carefully—she hobbled to the bathroom, washed her knees and hands—yelping between clenched teeth—and then bandaged the knees.

All the while, she thought of the curious kitten. Where did it sleep? She hoped not in the Dumpster. Once the ordeal of the knees was complete, she stiff-legged it back to her room and the beanbag. She pulled the backpack out of it and flopped down. A little kitten would love a beanbag like this. It would be like an entire planet to the small feline.

"You," she told herself severely, "do not have time to worry about wild cats. Do not be lazy. Ramp up your want-to." That was one of Dad's favorite lines. Heaving herself out of the beanbag and taking a quick glance at her room to make sure everything was in its place, she decided a snack before baked potatoes was necessary.

Downstairs, the kitchen island was littered with the contents of the fridge. Bill's head was deep within it.

"What are you doing?"

He sighed, backing out and straightening. "Looking for stuff to put on potatoes. Nutritional stuff for a healthy dinner. Your mother said."

She squinted a disbelieving look up at his six feet. "Like how much stuff do you want?" She shot a glance at the counter. "I don't think they grow potatoes big enough to hold all this."

Bill's laugh was as full as his smile. It began back in his throat, rolled up and out in a rich laugh that made you feel like you'd said something funny. And smart.

Taking the two steps to the island, she surveyed the piles. "Okay, let's start with what you don't need."

He closed the fridge door and sat on a stool across from her. He swept his arm magnanimously. "Go ahead. This counter looks like my workshop in the garage."

Vee had to agree, having peeked in the door once. She folded her arms and surveyed the excess. "I'd start with getting rid of the jar of peaches."

More Bill laughter. A tiny smile refused to hide inside Vee's face.

"Okay," he said. "Give me credit for that one. I just forgot to put it back in the fridge when I was after the pineapple."

The plastic container on the counter held pineapple tidbits left over from the cottage cheese and pineapple her mom ate every day for lunch. "You're going to put pineapple on a baked potato?"

Bill nodded, pulling another container toward the pineapple. "I was thinking that the potato could be like a pizza crust and we'd load pizza-topping-type stuff on it." He leaned forward over the leftover broccoli, the plastic bag of pepperoni, the hummus, a bunch of green onion, a red and green pepper, and a jar of olives and pulled the Canadian bacon package next to the pineapple. "See? A Hawaiian special potato. Whaddaya think?"

"I think there's a reason Mom cooks." She pushed the pineapple away, kept the Canadian bacon, and then pointed. "I'll eat *that* with butter and sour cream. And green onions. I'll put everything else back."

"Works for me!" Bill's face relaxed. "I think your mom would be cool with that."

Cool with that. Her dad never said that. Bill sometimes sounded like a kid. Wasn't he supposed to be the grown-up?

With Bill's head back in the fridge, Vee handed him the rejected potato toppings.

"So what happened that makes you look like you've run through a barbed-wire fence?" His voice sounded muffled deep in the recesses of the side-by-side fridge. "Oh. Your mom got a phone message from the school."

The retest, the curious kitten, Hermann and the Cat Woman, C. P., the service-learning project. For a moment, she wavered. *Trust Bill with a beetling day?* The next thought bopped the first one away. It was between her and Mom. Bill didn't fit in the spot for this problem. Laughing over dinner, yes, but not the big stuff.

Chapter 5

Have I Got a Deal for You

The sound of the garage door closing awoke Vee the next morning. Her first thought was the curious kitten. What did a Dumpster cat eat for breakfast? Maybe it was better if she didn't know. She rolled over to check her alarm clock. *Ye-ow!* Her tattered hands and knees protested loudly. Managing to roll to an upright position, she checked the clock: 6 a.m. Good. She'd have time to talk to her mother before she left for work. If the plan she'd made right before she fell asleep worked, Vee would not be heading for regular sixth grade.

After her Tuesday morning ritual of showering and conditioning her hair, she dried it and styled it into pigtails. She pulled on a pair of capris and a short-sleeve, long-waisted blouse she'd set out on the beanbag last night then slid everything she'd need into her backpack.

1. *Tell Mom the Plan.*
2. *Guidance counselor says Yes to the Plan.*
3. *Catch up on yesterday's math class work.*
4. *Keep want-to ramped up (eek!).*
5. *Tell girls the Plan.*

"Mom? . . ." On her way downstairs, she listened. "Oh, Mumseyyyyy!"

From the last step, she spotted the sheet of lined paper on the island counter. *Oh, beetle.* Her mother was gone *already*? She was glad her mom was one of the top Realtors in Oakton, but couldn't the *beetling* houses wait at least until her mother heard the Plan?

"Hey, little girl," her mother's scribbly handwriting ran. *"So sorry, baby, about the regular sixth grade. I'll be home early, and we'll go over your plans for the service-learning project the school mentioned. Bunches of hugs, Mumsey."* Her mom always signed her notes "Mumsey."

Slapping her head with one hand, Vee hustled to the fridge. Service-learning project. She remembered now that Mr. Tuttle had been talking about it when the guidance counselor hauled her off. She snagged a carton of yogurt, an apple, and a string cheese from the second shelf that she had convinced her mother and Bill should be her school lunch and after-school snack shelf. Closing the door with her foot, she added it to her backpack. Then, with the thought of the curious kitten peeking out at her yesterday, she grabbed a mini can of tuna with the pop-top lid her mom sometimes ate. Into the pack it went. "A little extra treat for you, curious kitten," she said to nobody.

Another moment and she'd neatly printed her response to her mother and was out the door for school.

> *Dear Mumsey,*
>   *TOP THREE THINGS FOR YOU to do TODAY*
>   *1. Talk to your daughter.*
>   *2. Talk to your daughter.*
>   *3. Talk to your daughter.*
>   *Love, Vee, who doesn't want to go to the BEETLING NORMAL SIXTH GRADE.*
>   *P.S. Beetling isn't a swear word. It's an interjection. I*

learned it in the ALC. See how important it is for me to stay in there? I need to talk to you!

The ALC seemed noisier this morning than the previous day. Fewer kids sat by themselves trying to look like they liked sitting by themselves. More were falling backward into the tub, laughing, sitting talking in the window seats, and generally no longer uneasy about a new school year.

Luckies.

The moment Mr. Tuttle closed the leader-citizen class, Vee dashed to the front of the room.

"Can I have a pass to the guidance office?"

He straightened from digging through the piles on his desk. "Can I help you with anything, Vee?"

She shook her head. "It's about yesterday."

For a moment he frowned, as though her *yesterday* hadn't registered on his radar. Then his face saddened. "I'll be sad to see you go, Vee."

"I'm not going," she said, taking the pass he handed her. "I have a plan."

She didn't even care if someone saw her running in the halls. She knocked on the office door. No answer. She knocked again and tried the handle. Locked. Good thing she'd come prepared with notebook and pen. She wrote:

Please give me time to study and retake the math part and stay in the ALC. I know I can do it. Yours very sincerely, Vee Nguyen.

Folding the note, she slipped it under the door.

Back in her seat in the ALC—oh, how she wanted it to continue to be her seat—Vee fished out the math book. Time to catch up. Where to start? Oh. The board. Each teacher placed their homework and any other notes on a white board that hung to the right of the big main board.

Ms. Smith: Review fractions. Chapter 1: Number Theory.
Complete divisibility exercise #1, Rational numbers #2.

Fractions. Vee hated fractions. They were stupid. Rational numbers? If there were rational numbers, were there irrational numbers? Irrational, like Dad said her dislike of the math tutor, Math Man, was? Inside, a super math zizzle zoomed around her stomach.

A hand was on her shoulder. Mr. Tuttle. This hand-on-the-shoulder bit was getting old. "Guidance counselor. In the hall." Another glance at the math book and Vee wasn't sure her note mattered. How could she understand seventh-grade math if last year's review zizzled her insides?

Regular sixth grade would be okay because:
1. *I would never have homework.*
2. *I can read while everyone else is finishing.*
3. *I might learn to understand math.*
4. *I'll be the smartest kid in the class.*

The guidance counselor held up the note. "I have your plan." She smiled. "Shall we talk?"

Should she go for the Plan? Vee hesitated.

What's WRONG with regular sixth grade:
1. *I lose my spot in the ALC, and then I don't have ANYTHING.*
2. *Kids in the regular class will think I wasn't smart enough to stay in the ALC.*

3. *I'll be bored.*
4. *I'll still have to do math.*
5. *C. P. will be in the ALC and I won't.*

The thought of the Squadders feeling sorry for her (except for maybe Esther, who secretly might be glad) rushed in. Bill and Mom. Spot. Dad and Heather. Spot. The Twin Terrors. Spot. Her. SPOT-LESS.

It did matter. She wanted—*needed*—her spot. It was the only place where she mattered. She so wanted to *matter*. Somewhere.

"Yes." This time her voice was firm. "My plan."

The guidance counselor gazed down the hall where two fifth-grade girls that Vee had seen at lunch were pushing an AV cart and taking turns jumping on the cart and riding it. She started to say something in that direction, shook her head, and turned back to Vee. "You are one of our most determined students, Vee," she said.

Vee's eyes filled quickly. Two tears spilled from her left eye and one from the right. "It's my spot," she whispered.

"Pretty much the first month is review, which just might give you the boost to push you over on the retake." The counselor appeared to be thinking out loud. "I've asked Ms. Smith. It's okay with her. Since that's the day the Helpful City Festival begins, there's no school. The festival won't open until noon, so you can take the retest in the morning. The charities looking for volunteers and vendors will be setting up their booths then. You can set up your service-learning project after the retest."

Sure. Whatever her service-learning project ended up *being*. Vee counted quickly. Just over a month. She could do this, pass the retest, and get back to the business of being one of the smart kids in the ALC.

Another hand on the shoulder. Did teachers learn this in teacher school? "Just don't put too much pressure on yourself, Vee. There's more to your sixth-grade year than being in the accelerated center. Lots of great kids are in the other sixth-grade class."

But Vee, while hearing, was not listening. Giddy with relief, she pushed open the door to the ALC, ignoring the doubt that popped up deep within her. She had a chance. She would win her spot.

Chapter 6

Good-bye, S.A.V.E. Squad

"What do you mean he's not home?" It was after seven.

Her stepmom Heather's voice flowed over the phone as warm as ever with a tiny hint of Southern twang. "Oh, baby, he's out of town for work."

"No, he can't be!" Vee's voice climbed to a shriek. She swallowed hard. "Can't I call his cell?"

"You could try to call, but it's one of those business retreats where everyone has to turn in their cell phone so they can truly engage, honey."

In the background Vee heard a crash and then two high-pitched voices shouting. She could never tell Joshua from Jacob and didn't really care to. They looked the same. They smelled the same. Like dirty feet and sweaty hair. Heather's voice turned away from the phone and said something muffled to the twins. Then she was back. "He'll be home for your weekend. He wants to see you."

Dad got to turn off his world? That was so *beetling* unfair.

"Can I help with anything, honey?" Her voice sounded hesitant.

Vee felt her face warm. She hadn't been too nice to Heather since her dad married her and her two kids. Mom had told her to be polite and she had, but—

"No. . .I guess. . .well, I want—need—to have Dad pay for math tutoring three times a week until the festival opens so I can pass the math readiness retake, otherwise I won't be able to stay in the accelerated but C. P. can and—"

"Whoa, whoa, that sounds like something your dad needs to do. Or your mom?"

Vee fell silent. Dad paid for math tutoring because Mom and Bill couldn't. Things had changed a lot since Mom and Dad divorced. Like Dad living in a really big house in the next town, and Mom and Vee in Bill's small house where the garage was bigger than the house.

"As long as I have you on the phone, Vee,"—her voice brightened—"how about you and me and the boys get together at Burger Mania so you three can have some bonding time?"

Bonding time. Burger Mania. The Twin Terrors. That *would* be mania. *No* thanks. As she moved to punch off the phone, she heard another crash in the background. She headed toward the stairs and the ATP that had her dad's number on speed dial. She knew him better than Heather did. He would never give up his cell phone. "I can do this! I just have to keep my want-to ramped up!" Her lips quivered, however, and the want-to was wanting to burst into ramped-up sobs.

The doorbell rang. She wanted to scream. Would the world just leave her alone? What else could go wrong? The tears she'd tried to swallow were falling. She'd just ignore the door. Bill breezed in from his garage. "Hey, Vee. I'll get the door. Your mom's working late again tonight. Leftovers okay?"

"Fine." She kept on going up the stairs. At the sound of a babble of familiar voices, she turned.

Bill stood with the front door open. Aneta, Sunny, and Esther surged through it, waving at Vee. She should tell them she was really busy. She didn't have time for friends right now. She needed to call her dad and get this day saved. Somehow. The idea of staring at that math book by herself until the retest spilled a couple more tears.

"We're here." Sunny grinned at her and then looked around the small living room. "Cool tree," she said of the floor-to-ceiling real potted palm Bill had gotten when he'd been flown to Hawaii to fix some special diesel engine before Vee's mom knew him.

"We are here," Aneta said quietly, her blue eyes shining. "We missed you on the library steps today."

Oh. The steps. They had made plans at the end of summer, during one of Aneta's Pool Plashes, that they would meet every day after school and walk home together. When they first met, they'd discovered they all lived within a street of each other, but since they all went to different schools, and Sunny homeschooled, they'd never met. Today she'd shot out of school like her backpack was on fire, sprinting to the community center parking lot.

The curious kitten had been on top of the Dumpster. As soon as Vee approached, all the cats vanished, including the curious one. She'd opened the little can, tucked it where the kitten seemed to like to peer at her, hoped for the best, and jetted home. A quick glance over her shoulder showed the curious kitten had found it. Their eyes met. Vee smiled.

"Sorry," she said to the girls, not knowing what else to say. Every second she stood there, her dad might be walking toward some stupid pile of stupid cell phones. *Don't do it, Dad!*

"Are you okay?" Esther cocked her head. "Your face looks funny. Have you been crying?"

A pause lay heavily between them until Bill shifted his feet and muttered, "Food. I'll get food," and disappeared into the kitchen.

Cupboard doors banged. Esther placed her hands on her hips and said, "We agreed we're not leaving until you tell us what's going on." She smiled a quick smile. "So there."

Fresh tears leaked as Vee regarded her three friends. The girls stepped forward and pulled her into the living room. Aneta knelt in front of Vee while Sunny and Esther flanked Vee on the sagging blue-green couch held up by old copies of *National Diesel Mechanics*.

Sunny patted her hand yet said nothing. Vee turned to her and found her red-haired friend's eyes sparkling, holding back the Sunny smile. Then it broke out.

"Vee," she said, flopping back against the couch and causing a couple of months of the magazines to slide, tipping her toward Vee. "What's wrong? You ditched us yesterday and today, and don't say you didn't." She grinned. "I'll just keep patting your hand like a grandma 'cause I don't know what's wrong."

Vee smiled a watery smile. Nobody could avoid smiling when Sunny did. Even Esther, who could get really crabby when other people were noticed, smiled when Sunny smiled.

"My mom said do not leave until you spill your. . .guts," Aneta said, slowly.

Unless Vee did, she'd never get to call her dad. She checked her thoughts. The girls cared. *Remember that.* Taking a deep breath, Vee sat up, squared her shoulders, and poured out the words: "There's the curious kitten. And my math score isn't high enough to stay in the Accelerated Learning Center, but C. P. can. If I pass a retest on the Friday morning when the Helpful City Festival starts, I can stay. This little curious one keeps looking at me—" She choked.

Her mother often said that "ventilating" made her feel better. Vee didn't feel better. In fact, she was perplexed. When had the welfare of the curious kitten risen to the same importance as staying in the ALC?

"I've got to call Dad on his cell phone before he puts it in the pile with the others—"

"Curious kitten in your ALC with C. P.?" Esther sounded confused. "Does your class have a class pet?"

"Food," Bill announced, coming through the kitchen doorway with a tray and three paper plates. Jagged chunks of yellow cheese and quartered apples lay on the plates. "Brain food. For whatever you need to figure out."

Esther dove in. "Wow, thank you, Mr.—" She paused and looked up at Bill, a piece of cheese in one hand and an apple quarter in the other. "Um, what's your name?"

"Bill." He departed.

"What I get is you need to retest in math?" Esther's voice sounded like she was puzzling out a mystery. Vee nodded.

"So you can stay in the ALC?" That was Aneta joining in.

Another nod.

"And it bugs you that C. P. doesn't have to retest to stay in the ALC," Sunny finished.

Vee hunched her shoulders and nodded.

"And the curious kitten comes in. . .?" Esther's voice rose in question. "I don't get that part."

Vee explained how she'd met the curious kitten and how she kept wondering about those Dumpster cats.

"They're wild cats," Sunny said. "The Cat Woman feeds them. What can we do?"

There had to be something to make Hermann not send the Animal Control officer to get rid of them. Whatever *get rid of* meant. It didn't sound good for the cats.

"I'm smart in math but not smarter than sixth grade," Esther said, folding her arms across her oversized T-shirt that read WHY NOT?

"Regular sixth grade isn't so bad, Vee. I'm having fun."

"My place is in the ALC. It has to be. My dad is out of town, and ole Heather won't tell the tutor to go ahead without Dad's permission."

For a few moments no one said anything.

Sunny stood up and began to pace in front of the coffee table. "Not to change the subject. . ." She pumped her arms like a windmill until her breath came in gasps. "But—to—change—whew!—the subject,"—she gestured to Esther and Aneta—"I guess all the teachers went to some conference this summer and heard service-learning projects were cool. My parents decided to have me do one with our homeschooling, too. We all chose projects that are at the senior center. Can you do yours there, too?"

There it was again. That *beetling* service-learning project. Their eager faces nearly undid her want-to to get to the phone.

"I—I. . ." Visions of leaving the ALC and reentering normal sixth grade danced in her head. "I can't think about a dumb service-learning project until I know I can stay in the ALC." She leaped to her feet. And figure out what to do about the curious kitten. "I have to keep my want-to ramped. It's me and the math book for the next month. Sorry."

She ushered the girls out the front door, hopping up and down on her toes, trying to bounce up some excitement, bouncing herself breathless instead. As the door closed behind the girls, she heard Aneta say, "Esther, I do not like a want-to ramp. It makes Vee not be with the Squad."

Oh, math. I hate you, you big beetle-y thing.

Twenty minutes later, she knew things were looking up. Dad had kept his phone. He had to whisper because he was hiding behind some tree so no one would see he still had his. Yes, he said, he'd call Math Man and authorize three times a week until the day before the retest.

"Dad, I know I can pass this test. I've got my want-to ramped up to the sky. I do!"

Her dad was quiet, and for a moment she thought someone had gotten to him and relieved him of his cell. "Okay," he said, finally. "When I get back, we need to talk about the want-to. Heather's been talking to me about that and I—"

Yes, yes, yes. He'd said yes. She'd show him. A Dad Weekend was coming up, and even though she'd probably have to shout above the Twin Terrors yelling and breaking things, she'd explain how important it was to stay in the ALC. He could give her some ideas on how to help the curious kitten. "Sure, Dad. See you this weekend. Bye!"

Chapter 7

Beetle-y Math Man

Vee sighed, wrenching her gaze away from the sliding glass door and her dad and the Twin Terrors playing soccer in the backyard. She was supposed to have Dad all to herself on Dad Weekends. Already it was late Saturday afternoon, and she'd still not gotten her father alone.

"Focus, Vee," came the voice she despised. Math Man looked rather like a beetle with his short neck and eyebrows that winged out like antennas. She bent her head over her paper and pencil again, wondering if beetles had bad breath.

"Sorry," she muttered. She stared at the word problem.

During a winter's night, the lowest temperature was recorded at 19 degrees Fahrenheit. The wind-chill factor that same night was -7 degrees Fahrenheit. What was the difference between the wind-chill temperature and the low temperature?

It wasn't winter, first off. Vee hated word problems that didn't have anything to do with real life. She penciled in *12* and moved on.

What is the common difference of the arithmetic pattern shown here: -5, -1, 3, 7, . . .

Vee's pencil began to doodle a stick figure of a kitten in the margins of the page. Twenty-six days from today until the retest. She would be stuck with Math Man forever. Sighing, she snuck another look at the yard. The Twin Terrors had just tackled Dad around the knees, and he was struggling to walk. And laughing.

Math Man checked his watch. "Our hour is up. You've got all the tools to get this math down. I don't know why it's not clicking for you. I haven't had this trouble with other students." His tone wondered as though maybe Vee was the first idiot he'd ever tutored. Her ears burned.

What to do after passing retest:
Have a party

Math Man left to talk to her father while Vee packed up her backpack. She slanted a glance out of the corner of her eyes to see if she could tell what was going on. Math Man was gesturing with his long, skinny arms, his ever-present black coat flapping a little. Dad sent the Twin Terrors into the house. That ended any kind of spying.

"Hi, Vee the B!" said Twin Terror number one or TT1. He was an exact copy of his little brother and couldn't have looked less like Vee. They were blond, their thick hair longish and always in their eyes. Vee wanted to get rubber bands and tie their hair up like a Yorkie terrier. It would be safer to see their not-so-innocent eyes. With big brown eyes, they looked sort of like those cherubs on the Victorian Christmas cards her grandmother sent. Any resemblance ended there. They were loud and smelled like boys who hated baths.

TT2 flopped into a chair next to her. "Vee the B. That creepy guy told Papa you won't pass the test even if you stand on your head." Flailing his arms, he fell off the chair and rolled up against the wall where he tried to stand on his head, banging his feet on the wall as he flung them up time after time.

"Get your feet off the wall," Vee said, putting her backpack by the stairs to take up to her room. *Thanks a lot, Math Man.*

Heather breezed into the kitchen, her signature perfume of something citrusy wafting over to Vee. Vee sniffed. It was a vital antidote to O'dor de Boys.

"Boys, leave Vee alone. You're not to torment." Her Southern twang took on flecks of ice when she was stern. "Joshua, get your feet off the wall."

Behind her back, Vee made a "ha-ha" face. So that one was Joshua. How did their mother tell? Vee had to give her stepmother credit, however grudgingly. She didn't let the Twin Terrors get away with much. Dad did though. Like he was trying to be their friend or something.

After Math Man left and the Twin Terrors set a table of crooked silverware, Vee brought out the big pasta bowl of fettuccine. Heather followed with an equally large pitcher of Alfredo sauce. After dashing back to the kitchen for the broccoli, Heather joined them at the table and held out each of her hands to the Twin Terrors who flanked her. Vee sat by her dad and TT1, the mouth breather.

Eating dinner at Dad's house meant listening to the stepbrother talk with his mouth full while he tried to breathe. Dad said Vee needed to not tell him every five minutes to close his yap. Bill said yap. Vee liked the sound of the word. A beetling *yap* open at dinner. She took the sticky, sweaty hand, trying not to grimace. Dad squeezed her other hand, and when she turned to smile at him, he winked. *Oh, Dad.*

Heather bowed her head, "Thank You, Lord, for the food we are about to eat. Help us find our place in You every moment."

With all the horrible changes, Heather blessing the food was one addition Vee liked. It reminded Vee of Sunny and Esther who talked to God like He was their friend, only lots bigger. Tonight part of the familiar prayer sounded as loud as one of the Twin Terror's fights: *"Help us find our place in You every moment."* She was sure her spot was in the ALC.

> *What I need:*
> 1. *More tutoring sessions with Math Man (ick).*
> 2. *Doing extra homework (double ick).*
> 3. *God to turn the fire alarm sprinklers on and ruin the math test.*

The last one? Okay, maybe not. In her mind, she drew a single line through it. They would just print out another test. Unless, of course, the sprinklers ruined the printer, too. . . .

After dinner Dad walked by and patted her shoulder. "How about a walk? Heather wants the boys to help with cleaning up after dinner so you and I can have some no-boy time. Sound good?"

Evening still held off these days, letting the day stay warm and long. From the moment they hit the driveway and headed down the cul-de-sac of huge houses, it seemed like she couldn't shut off her mouth. She talked about the Squad coming over and how she wanted to work with them at the senior center but couldn't because she had to pass this retest. She talked about the curious kitten and how they'd discovered each other in the bushes. She talked about the language arts teacher and *beetle*. Dad laughed loudly at that and threw his arm around her shoulder.

"Vee, you are so funny. I bet your teacher loves having you in class."

Vee felt like a spotlight had been lit inside. Talking about the girls made her want to be with them. Surely they knew what she had to give up to stay in the ALC. It would only be twenty-six days. Just until the Friday morning of the Helpful City Festival.

"I really like the Accelerated Learning Center, Dad. My want-to is going strong—"

"Your mom called while you and Heather were finishing up the sauce," Dad interrupted. Anybody who had known Dad for even a little time knew he thought in "rooms." And when he was in one room, he didn't hear you talking from another room. He was in the Mom Phone Call Room.

"Dad, this is important. It's so cool in the ALC. There's a big bathtub and—"

"Shall we do a little jog and burn off some dinner?" Dad increased his pace until Vee moved to an effortless trot. She gave up and began to grin. The smile on her face felt silly, like she was some little kid, but she couldn't help it. She and Dad used to run together several times a week since she was little.

"I'll race you to the tree with the sign on it!" she yelled and took off.

"Hey, no fair! You're getting a head start." She heard a laugh in his voice.

"Ramp up your want-to, Dad!" She pressed her hands at her sides, hands open and straight. Pump, pump. Her knees rose and fell. The tree got nearer. Footsteps pounded behind her, and she puffed out short bursts of breath. Just. A. Few. More. Feet.

"Passing!" Dad yelled and blew past her, reaching the tree seconds before her. Vee groaned and plowed into him, wrapping her arms around him. "Just 'cause your legs are longer!"

A Good Dad Weekend:
1. *No Math Man*
2. *No Twin Terrors*
3. *Run with Dad*

She pushed off her father's stomach and turned to face him, hands on hips. "You almost didn't beat me. You haven't been running, have you?"

"Boys like soccer, not running. Heather goes to the gym. Vee, about that 'want to. . .'" He moved from the tree and back onto the sidewalk where they continued, still both a little out of breath. "It's not always—well—" He seemed to change his mind, shaking his head, and then went back to the Mom Phone Call Room. "Your mom wants you and me to come up with a service-learning project. She says you've been procrastinating?" He turned to look at her. "That's not like you, Veelie." He only called her Veelie when he was worried. He flung his arm over her shoulder, rocking her off balance and into his side. "I have a suggestion for your service-learning project."

A quiver of excitement wriggled up Vee's spine. "Great! With you?"

"Yeah," he said. "I've decided to coach the boys' soccer team, and we need a statistician. It would be a great way to practice math and be with me and the boys. Help us spend some family time."

Chapter 8

Just *What* Is Going on Here?

"Oh look! Your Dumpster cats, Vee." Sunny pointed toward six felines, all shades and stripes of gray, black, and white, who loitered in and out of the bushes and on the Dumpster.

Vee stretched on the stairs, watching the curious kitten play with some kind of crawling bug over by the Dumpster. Bugs. She shivered and flexed her feet. "I can't understand why old Hermann wants to get rid of them. And what does he mean by getting 'rid' of them?"

"Hermann's old. Maybe he'll forget he wants to do that," Esther suggested. "Okay, girls, time to sign in for our projects."

Groans from everyone.

"I do not like the smell of chicken." Aneta pulled her hair off her neck and twisted it into a knot.

"I do not like handing Frank tools," Sunny joined in.

"I do not like old ladies telling me ninety jillion times how to up-load pictures to the website for the Helpful City Festival," Esther complained.

"I do not like sorting and scanning photographs." Vee laughed with the girls. After Dad's *ultim-o-horrible* suggestion that she be the numbers keeper on Saturday, she had volunteered for anything upon entering the ALC today. Now she wished Mr. Tuttle had picked something more interesting for her.

Esther pulled an "I'm sorry" face. "Aneta, I heard the kitchen lady say you were cutting onions for lunch tomorrow."

At Esther's comment, Aneta made a face, stood, and pushed her hair behind her ears. "I will cry, cry, cry," she said, making an equally pretend sobbing face.

Vee sprang to her feet. "I have to be home for Math Man in two hours. I better get going with my sorting and scanning. What are we supposed to learn from these projects anyway?" She stretched. "If I'm late twice or a no-show, ole Math Man will kick me off his list and it's good-bye ALC."

"We are good workers," Aneta said, sounding a little anxious. Vee knew her friend had a tendency to worry about doing the right thing.

"Even if our projects are screaming boring," Sunny added.

Vee trotted into the building. Almost two hours of photo boxes. *Geesh.*

At the end of her time, balancing three boxes of photos that had been combed through and scanned, Vee staggered down the hall toward the arts and crafts room where she had been promised the closet had been cleaned out and was ready for more stuff. What did they need to keep old photos for anyway? Who was going to look at them stashed in a closet? She felt a sneeze coming on and slowed, trying to keep the big boxes steady.

The enormous man had said she should only take one box at a time, but that would mean going back for two more trips. She would then cut it too close to make it home for Math Man. So she had insisted the enormous man place two *small* boxes on top of the first one. His idea of small and hers were different. She felt the boxes slip.

The sneeze tickled again. So did thoughts of whether to set down the boxes and just sneeze. Then she might not be able to pick them up again. That would make her really late. What if she sneezed with the boxes? Would she fall down and not be able to get up and *still* be late? Trying to breathe deeply and thwart the sneeze, she smelled burning onions. And smoke.

"Oh! Oh! Oh!" Aneta's voice, rising to a shriek, came in loud and clear as Vee neared the kitchen.

"Help! Fire!" came Sunny's voice from somewhere. The next moment, something hit Vee behind the knees, and she flew forward. Only it wasn't like she'd ever expected flying to be. Rather, she leap-frogged awkwardly into the air, letting go of the boxes, collapsing on her hands and knees. Right before a wheelchair ran over her, pinning her to the floor.

"Yikes! Sorry! Sorry!" It was Sunny's voice again.

The boxes, released into flight, moved like a slo-mo commercial—bashing into Esther who had stepped out of the audio-visual room with an old lady. The stocky girl tipped over like a bowling pin on Family Fun Night. A grunt escaped her. Vee winced. Those boxes were heavy.

Trying to get her brain to remember where her legs and arms were so she could stand up and help Aneta, who was still screaming, and somehow stop the smoke that still poured out of the kitchen, Vee thought of Math Man. She could not be late. But it was more important that she find out if Sunny was hurt. Was Esther okay? Wasn't anyone going to stop that smoke? *Beetle!* How much worse could it get?

"Just what is going on here?" A sharp voice punched through the chaotic yelling and groaning.

Vee peered up at the senior center director standing with Hermann, and the Animal Control officer. Oh, it could get plenty worse.

Chapter 9

Where's the Curious Kitten?

The next day, as Vee approached what she considered "Squad" steps after school, she looked at the Dumpster. About half the cats were lying on the lid of the Dumpster in the sun. There was no sight of the curious kitten. Something clutched in her stomach.

Arriving late for Math Man after the disaster at the senior center yesterday, he'd yapped about how she had one time left to be late. Vee, explaining that it had been a matter of life and death with smoke and onions and wheelchairs and murderous boxes and the really mad senior center director, hadn't moved Math Man.

The Squad hadn't talked to each other last night. That meant everyone was either busy or in trouble for getting kicked out of the senior center. Or both. With Vee, it had been both. Her mother had called her dad; both had said they were disappointed in her and they hoped she would use better judgment in the future. And of course, there was math homework.

The girls were there already, sitting off to the side of the library steps, as far away from the senior center as you could get and still be at the community center.

Esther leaned back on her elbows. Vee saw her point toward the Dumpster. That Cat Woman was there, preparing her pie pans of kitty food.

"Have you seen the curious kitten?" Vee asked, dropping down next to Esther.

Sunny turned toward the Dumpster. "You mean your under-the-bush buddy? Nope. Looks like some others are missing, too."

"You don't think the Animal Control officer got them already, do you?" Vee remembered the Animal Control officer in the senior center yesterday.

"Don't worry." Esther stretched out her solid legs on the step below. "Don't you think we would've heard Cat Woman if he was doing that?"

"Hmmm," was all Vee said.

After a few moments of quietly watching the cats, Vee started the conversation they were all avoiding. "You won't believe what my mother is making me do."

"What?" Aneta asked.

"My mom says I have to find a new project at the senior center." Vee waited for the girls to freak that Mom was making Vee go back to where certain death awaited.

Sunny halted her spinning and staggered in a circle. "You're kidding. So did mine."

Aneta said, "My mom said it would be a redemption, whatever that means."

Esther began laughing. "Mine, *too*. It's never good for us when they start talking."

"How can we go back in there? They hate us!" Vee's voice was loud.

A long, large car, the kind that old people drive, pulled into the community center parking lot. Hermann slowly climbed out, slamming the door. Two Dumpster cats shot past his feet.

"Kots!" He said. He looked at the girls. "Kids!" he said.

Moments later, they stood outside the senior center director's door.

"You knock on her door." Sunny nudged Esther.

Esther backed up. "No, you. She likes you better."

Are you nuts? She doesn't like any of us. Vee hung back.

Sunny whispered, "Yeah, but she didn't see Esther do anything."

Aneta frowned. "We didn't *do* anything. It all just *happened*."

"True," Vee said. "Esther, you knock on the door."

"I'm glad I'm good for something, since you guys got me in trouble."

"We didn't mean to get you in trouble," Sunny said, giving Esther a quick hug and darting back. "You just stuck your head out the door and *wham*—"

"Yeah." Esther tapped on the office door then rubbed her shoulder. "*Wham*. I'm injured for life." No answer. She knocked again, harder.

The door swung inward. The director, a tall, dark-haired woman who looked as if she would schedule when to smile into her monthly to-do list, looked down at the girls. "I am in a meeting with the mayor." She moved to close the door.

Good, thought Vee. *The mayor likes us.* She brushed past Esther. "Hi. We came to apologize for the um. . .things. . .that happened."

The director's sour-candy-sucking expression didn't change. "You girls certainly know how to disrupt an entire building. We've never had such volunteers."

"Girls?" said a familiar voice from behind her. The short mayor, who only came to the director's shoulder, peered around the larger woman. "Why, hello, S.A.V.E. Squad! Sissy was just telling me about the mishap." She broke into a wide grin. "You certainly shook things up around here!"

Sissy? Vee started to grin. The director so did not look like a Sissy. A tall dwarf, like Grumpy, maybe, but not a Sissy.

"We are not in need of being shook up," Mrs. Sissy said between her teeth.

The mayor stepped around her and out into the hall. "My sister isn't a big fan of change."

Sister? Weirder and weirder. The two ladies didn't look at all alike. Kind of like herself and the Twin Terrors.

Vee seized her chance. "We're here to ask if we could still finish our service-learning project here at the senior center."

Behind the mayor, the director seemed to swell. "To cause more trouble? I don't think so." She waved her arm at them. "I accept your apology, but returning is not an option."

The mayor, however, patted Vee on the shoulder and began to usher the girls toward the door. "Of course, Sissy."

"Don't call me Sissy. It's unprofessional."

The mayor escorted the girls out of the building and onto the steps in the sunshine. There she stopped and folded her arms across her ample chest.

"So what's your plan, girls? My sister is pretty tough to convince."

"I—we—" Vee tripped over her tongue and flung an agonized look at the girls. They opened their mouths with the same result.

She didn't need this in combination with studying for the all-important math retest. A simple job, please. One to make her mom and dad and Mr. Tuttle happy. Her gaze flickered over at movement out of the corner of her eye. The curious kitten was back! Hermann hadn't succeeded yet. The mom cat and curious kitten were back; the kitten was wavering on the corner of the opened container.

As Vee watched, listening to the girls suggest projects like *yard work*—ew—the kitten wobbled fiercely, uttered a tiny squeal Vee heard across the parking lot, and, scrabbling for a foothold, fell into the Dumpster.

In the next breath, Vee heard the roar of the garbage truck as it pulled into the parking lot.

Chapter 10

Diving In

A string of cats streaked for the bushes.

Vee sort of saw the mayor and the girls' faces when she screamed, "Oh, no!" and then dashed across the lot, trying to catch up with the truck as it rumbled past her, the driver nodding his head to what Vee supposed must be the radio.

"Hey!" she shouted, making it to the door and leaping up to pound on it. She heard the mayor's horrified shriek and the girls' screams. She knew the girls were on their way with the footsteps sounding behind her, but would any of them get there in time? The driver neared the bin where his claws of death would reach down, snatch the Dumpster with the curious kitten lost in garbage, raise it up, and—

Putting on the speed her dad called "the Vee sprint," she darted in front of the truck. As she passed its grill, she noted the dead moths in it. *I hope I'm not the latest decoration.* Flapping her hands wildly, she flung a desperate look at the driver whose eyes bulged at her presence. He jerked back in his seat. The brakes squealed. The truck continued to roll. Would she get to the Dumpster before the truck flattened her? A hard bump hit her right leg. It went numb. She slammed into the Dumpster.

That would leave a mark.

She reached up, grabbed the side of the Dumpster, and bounced on the good leg. Hard.

Plan:
1. *Bounce*
2. *Sling leg over rim*
3. *Grab kitten*
4. *Jump down*

Using the momentum, she hovered halfway over the Dumpster rim. In the next second, she knew to her deepest chagrin that the principle of momentum she'd learned this week in science was going to take her farther than she wanted to go. She was going Dumpster diving whether she wanted to or not. Head. First.

Beetle!

Chapter 11

Operation Catness

It was crazy. The truck hits you, we scream. The mayor gets on the phone with 911." Sunny was chattering as Vee sat with a blanket around her—sweating—and the paramedic shined a light in her eyes and asked her to follow his fingers. Frank had joined the bunch of people hovering around Vee. He was shaking his head. Vee knew what he was thinking: *drama.*

"The curious kitten!" She threw off the blanket. Ouch. That hip was sore. *I really raced a garbage truck. And lost. Unbelievable.*

Esther pushed her down gently. "That driver thought he'd mushed you. He didn't see you dive into the Dumpster—" She leaned in and sniffed. "Yep. Pretty gross with it being a hot day and all."

Slimy. Vee's word for the day. Something glued her armpit together. And *sticky.*

Aneta finished the story. "We see nothing first. We do not know if you are, are. . . Then you put your arm up. The kitten is in it!" She reached forward and hugged Vee then ducked away with a face. "The kitten scratches you and runs away. You are safe. You smell bad." She brushed something off her shirt.

"You're a hero," Sunny said, flopping down next to her as the paramedic moved away to the mayor who was lacing and unlacing her hands. "And boy, can you run fast!"

Vee glanced over at the mayor. Her Dumpster dive had ruined any chance of the girls returning to the senior center. Since the first day of school she'd been apologizing. Every plan that worked before wasn't working now. Her eyes widened; she dropped the blanket and stood up, keeping the weight off her right hip.

That crazy curious kitten was peeking at her from under the Dumpster the truck had just thudded down before it roared off. Right back into danger. Vee breathed out a pent-up breath. She approached the mayor.

"I am so—," she began, reaching up a damp hand—*what was that drooling down her arm?* It was green and not pretty. She sensed rather than saw the girls around her. "I want to save these Dumpster cats for my service-learning project. Give them a spot."

The mayor's sister looked relieved. "That's just fine. You do that." An almost-smile crept across her face. "It will keep you out of my senior center."

"Yes! The S.A.V.E. Squad saving their catness. Operation Catness!" Sunny spun in circles with delight. Staggering a bit she continued, "We'll all do it, won't we!" She looked at Esther and Aneta, who nodded enthusiastically.

"Squad bracelets united!" Esther stepped forward and put out her wrist with the leather string and beads the girls had created after their first adventure.

"Yes! We'll save the Dumpster cats and find homes for them all!" Sunny touched her wrist to Esther's. Vee added her bracelet. Aneta followed suit.

Vee scanned them with a *thank-you* look. How hard could it be to find homes for cats this cute? She'd save the curious kitten and more and still have time to study for the retest.

"From what I count in and around that Dumpster, that's six cats," the mayor said, looking less than impressed. "That's not much of a project for super-talented Junior Event Planners like you girls. I have an idea."

Uh-oh. Simple job. Just a simple service-learning project. Please.

"Oh, girls! Sissy, I know you're going to love it." The mayor threw an arm around her larger sibling. Mrs. Sissy didn't look like she was going to love anything her shorter, dynamic sister had to say.

Everyone stepped back to the senior center steps.

The mayor looked at her sister. "What is your primary goal between now and the end of October?"

Her sister looked aggrieved. "You know as well as I do. Win the Helpful City Festival contest. Show Oakton has the best volunteers and helpful programs for its citizens."

"*I* envision our Helpful City Festival working toward the contest by connecting disparate populations, our youths and our seniors," the mayor said.

Vee made a note to look up *disparate*. It sounded scary. "I envision a lot of work," she muttered. A giggle escaped Sunny. Vee stole another look toward the Dumpster. The curious kitten sat washing its face, watching Vee. Yes, she wanted to give the curious kitten a spot. She did *not* want to become an event in the mayor's Helpful City Festival.

The mayor turned to Frank, who was looking at his phone. She nudged him. "Frank, you'd be great to supervise the girls. Sissy,"—she hugged her sister—"you want to win this Helpful City Contest. I just gave you an easy way to be different." She beamed at everyone, waggled her fingers again, and headed toward her car in the parking lot. "Vee, just zip me an e-mail when you come up with your ideas. I am totally supportive!"

The girls traded looks. Vee and the curious kitten traded looks. *It is no longer just finding you a spot.* Vee sent the thoughts the kitten's way. It's turned into a *beetling* great cat caper.

Chapter 12

Oh No, You're Not!

School was pretty much a blur the rest of the week with the girls arguing over how to save the cats. Even language arts, which was usually unforgettable. On Friday, at lunch, the kids at the table waved their hands in front of Vee when she looked right through them. C. P. said she had cat fever. One of the kids wanted to know if it was contagious. She remembered *that*. Dumb.

Soon, however, their saving cats would be complete. As she jogged toward the community center for Operation Catness, her backpack banged against her back. *Ouch. Ouch. Ouch.* In her head, she recited the plan they'd finally agreed on:

Operation Catness:
1. *Open the tuna cans.*
2. *Catch the curious kitten first then the others.*
3. *Give them to Frank and Nadine.*
4. *Get home to tutoring.*
5. *Make a sign-up sheet for people to adopt the cats.*
6. *Be done.*

It would take about an hour and a half to catch the momma cat, the kittens, and the three other grown cats. After the handoff to Nadine and Frank, she would buzz on home and get the math tutoring over with. Then Mom would order pizza, and she, Bill, and Mom would watch a movie during dinner. Then Dad would pick her up for the weekend.

Maybe on Sunday she could pop over and see the curious kitten at Frank and Nadine's. Monday, the Squad would have to come up with the additional ideas the mayor would like. She remembered their first adventure. Four girls with nothing in common but their differences. Now they were fast friends, even if they still sometimes disagreed. Ideas would come quickly. End of trouble.

As she approached the senior center and saw the girls streaming from different directions, converging toward the steps, she laughed. Operation Catness begins! Sunny rolled in on her knobby-tire bike with her messenger bag slung across her shoulders. Aneta lugged a canvas bag; Esther tipped off her blue backpack with her school's name emblazoned across it.

"Are we ready?" Vee reviewed the list with the girls. "Let's start Operation Catness!"

Aneta looked hesitant. "Do we need Frank to be here?" She glanced over at the Dumpster. So did Vee. Not a cat to be seen. That was okay.

"Once we open the cans of tuna, they will come running. It happens in all the cat food commercials." Vee hoped the curious kitten would pick her can first.

Sunny shrugged. "I bet the mayor just wanted Frank to be in on the project so he could drive us if we need it. You know, because it's a senior center project and all, and he's the senior center driver."

"What about the Cat Woman?" Esther stuck her hands on her hips. "I think we're moving too fast. I think we should have her here to help us. I mean, what do we know about Dumpster cats?"

Vee felt her familiar impatience rising with Esther. That girl seemed to get going in the opposite direction every time Vee came up with a plan. Didn't Esther remember Vee needed to study for this retest and couldn't spend all day tracking down Frank? "What's so hard about catching cats?" she asked. "I've watched the Cat Woman feed them a couple of times. She sets the food out and steps aside. Only this time, when they're eating, we'll slowly move in and pick them up."

Unflapping her canvas messenger bag, Aneta withdrew several cans of tuna. Esther and Sunny did the same with their bags, giggling as the pile of canned tuna grew. Vee added hers to the pile.

"Okay, I think we should open the cans here and then put them on the plates like the Cat Woman does," Vee said, inspecting the pile of tuna with pride. There was enough tuna to feed two cities' Dumpster cats. Operation Catness was a great plan.

"Umm—" It was Sunny smothering a giggle.

Vee raised her gaze. "What?"

"Can opener? Pie plates?"

The *stellar* leaked out of her plan like air out of a balloon that had the misfortune to fall into the Twin Terrors' hands. How could she forget to put those on her list? Lists were her specialty. She *thought* in lists. They were what got her into the accelerated class. She chewed the inside of her lip. Tutoring three times a week along with everything else was messing up her brain.

"There's an opener in the senior center kitchen." Aneta shoved her hands into her skirt pockets. "But I do not want to go in there."

The girls looked at one another.

Finally Vee sighed. "Okay, I'll go in and ask." On the way in, she could feel the girls' eyes boring into her and tried to make her steps jaunty, like she wasn't afraid of (1) Mrs. Sissy, (2) the cook Aneta helped on the day of the fire, or (3) Hermann, if he found out the girls had cut short his plan to get rid of the cats.

Once inside, Vee blinked to adjust from the brightness. As she passed a tired-looking brown-and-gray-haired woman, the woman ducked away from her like Vee had reached out and bit her. A medicine-y mouthwash smell about blew Vee over as the woman passed, hugging the wall.

Whew.

In the kitchen she found a friendly face. "That's a hard task you've given yourselves, and I don't mean maybe," the woman said. Vee smiled and took the proffered can opener, promising to bring it right back. She also accepted four pie pans and headed out the door with a light heart. Operation Catness was again proving stellar!

Two more steps, then *WHAM.* She ran smack into the Cat Woman. Since they were the same height, their foreheads banged. *That* kind of smacked. Vee shoved out her arms to keep the woman from falling but ended up pushing her down with the pie pans. They clattered loudly on the corridor, along with the can opener at the same moment as Mrs. Sissy walked out the door across the way. Hermann was with her.

Mrs. Sissy leaped forward to help the Cat Woman, pushing away Vee's assistance. "What are you up to now?" she cried. "Pushing down helpless old women?"

Vee remembered Sunny telling her they were not allowed to call the seniors "old." It did not, however, seem a good time to remind Mrs. Sissy.

Hermann set the Cat Woman on her feet. Then the two turned and regarded Vee. Hermann's face set in hard lines. Vee's face flamed like a bad sunburn. She knelt and picked up the can opener and pans.

"I forgot the can opener and pie pans," she said, her words jerking a bit over her madly beating heart. Honestly, you'd think she'd knocked over Cat Woman *on purpose.*

Hermann grunted. "Kots und kids. Bah! You tink you got und easy job. Yah! My way is better. You vill see."

If people would just leave them alone, they would get this project finished and get those cats into good spots. Hermann would see. She shifted impatiently, sneaking a look at her watch. No way was she going to be late a second time for Math Man.

"You!" Cat Woman huffed and straightened her velour running jacket, which, Vee noticed, was covered in cat hair. She suddenly remembered where she'd first seen the woman. During the girls' first adventure, she'd been the woman who wouldn't stop talking about her cats when they stopped at her door with an important mission. She opened her mouth to say more when Frank joined the group.

His gaze took in the can opener and the pie pans then went up to Vee. His eyebrows slanted together. She remembered Aneta's comment, "Do we need Frank here?" From the indignant expression on his face, *yes.*

"What happened to including the project supervisor in your little project?" he asked, folding long, skinny arms over an equally skinny chest.

"Hey, you!" It was the friendliest voice so far. Nadine walked up to her husband and slid an arm around his waist. She smiled at Vee. "Whatcha up to?"

"Our project," Vee stammered. "We're going to catch the cats to start our project."

A heavy silence sucked the oxygen out of the corridor before four voices chorused, "Oh no, you're not!"

An hour later Vee and the girls stood shaking their heads.

"Who knew?" Sunny said.

"Not us," Aneta said.

"We messed up big-time," Esther said.

Nothing is going right, Vee agreed.

Chapter 13

Caught in a Trap

They listened to the unhappy cats in the sheet-covered traps.

"I am so glad I smacked into the Cat Woman," Vee said.

The girls gave her the stink eye.

"I mean, in a good way. She had the traps in the senior center closet. Weird."

1. *You need special traps to trap Dumpster cats.*
2. *You might not catch them all (one got away).*
3. *Dumpster cats do NOT think you are helping them.*
4. *Dumpster cats make scary monster noises when they are not happy.*
5. *Sheets are required.*
6. *When Frank gets mad, his face gets blotchy.*

Sunny started to giggle. "The Cat Woman told us to cover the traps with sheets so the cats can begin to de-stress. Maybe we need to put a sheet over Frank."

Frank had his head tipped back as though speaking to God. "I survived the first time with these four. Wasn't that enough? Like I need the drama again?"

Vee wished the parking lot would swallow her up. How was she supposed to know that there was training involved to do this project?

Sunny swallowed her giggles and walked up to Frank. "Oh, Frank, I'm sorry. I think—" She paused and looked at Vee, who had a suspicious feeling Sunny was thinking Vee should be saying what she said next. "We didn't think this through."

Frank stomped into the senior center, passing Hermann who made a disgusted face at the traps, climbed into his car, and drove off.

"Frank is mad at us," Aneta observed. "Hermann thinks our plan is terrible."

Nadine finished inspecting the covered traps and approached the group. She blew out a breath. "I'm thinking you girls got carried away by your success in your first adventure."

A rush of anger surged up from deep within Vee. She'd gotten her want-to ramped up to volunteer to save Dumpster cats nobody wanted. Hadn't she offered her time when *everybody*—well, maybe not Nadine and Frank and Cat Woman and Hermann or Mrs. Sissy—but everyone *else* knew she was hitting the math books so hard they were hitting back. Not only that, she and the Squad—and *her* lists—were going to come up with ideas for the mayor's beetle-y Helpful City Festival. The lists would be stellar, um, when she made some. Wasn't that enough?

"We sure did," Esther said. She shot a look at Vee. "I said we were rushing catching the cats."

Cat Woman, standing like her spine was made of steel, snapped, "You got that right, and you still don't have it right. You don't *catch* community and stray cats. You have to *trap* them. What were you planning to do, sneak up on them while they were eating and invite them to jump into your pocket?"

Nadine held up her hands like a referee. "Okay, let's get some perspective here. Would you girls agree that it would have helped the cats if you had thought this out better?"

Even while her mind was saying *yeah, but,* she heard her voice say yes along with the others. Her time to help was up for today. A piteous meow sounded from the curious kitten's trap. She did want the curious kitten to find a spot. *With me.* The new, tiny thought jabbed her so hard she jumped.

Cat Woman humphed. "I've seen what do-gooders do. They don't want to learn. They just want to do something fast and have people tell them they're wonderful for helping the animals."

Vee's face warmed. "I have to go home now to meet the tutor. Then my dad's picking me up for the weekend."

Nadine appeared lost in thought, then as the girls started their good-byes, picking up messenger bags and backpacks, she began to walk toward her Toyota. "Sure, Vee. Good luck with your tutoring. Great job, girls. Be sure to keep Frank in the loop for the next step!" she called.

"Next step?" Sunny whipped her head to stare at Vee, mouth wide open. "Vee! She's leaving."

Aneta murmured something that sounded like, "Okay, God, now what do we do?"

Esther ran after Nadine. "Nadine! You forgot the cats!"

Nadine turned around and walked backward, her tanned face still smiling. "No, you've got all the plans."

Yes, and that plan was to give the cats to Nadine and get home to Math Man *on time.* "Wait! Wait!" Vee chased after the two women. She had fifteen minutes to get home before Math Man showed up. "You can't just *leave* them here with *us.*"

Chapter 14

Panic Time

Frank walked out the senior center door, glanced at the cat carriers and then at the girls. Esther stood, hands on hips. Aneta crouched by the traps, murmuring. Sunny bounced up and down, first looking at Nadine and Gladys, then at Frank and the girls. Frank watched his wife's back. Suddenly he looked much more cheerful. Vee could not think why. This was *serious*.

Stuffing his hands in his pockets, he passed each girl with a nod. "Let's talk Monday on how it goes this weekend, okay? We still have to figure out what the other events are going to be."

"Frank!" Esther was trying to sound bossy and only sounded scared.

"You cannot leave! The cats!" Aneta's voice had tears in it.

"You guys! Don't go!" Sunny stood absolutely still.

Frank opened the door behind the driver's side for Gladys. She stiffly bent and got in. Then he went around to open the door for his wife, who stood on her toes and whispered something in her husband's ear. Then he was in the car. They really were going to leave them alone with the cats.

Vee ran to the car and pounded on the window. "Frank! Don't leave us here." Terror ramped up her want-to. "WE DON'T HAVE A PLAN!"

The girls pressed up against her. "Frank, you gotta help us!" Sunny yelled.

Frank rolled the window down.

Aneta whimpered.

"You sure you need help?"

"Yes!" the girls shrieked.

Frank said, "Go get the carriers. I will take them home with us *for one night.*"

The girls dashed off and returned carefully carrying the traps of the hissing, growling, unhappy cats. Frank got out of the car and placed the carriers around Gladys in the back and one on her lap. She clutched it, dipping her head to give the girls the stink eye. Nadine jumped out and took the last cage from Vee.

Now Vee had less than ten minutes to run home.

As soon as Nadine was in the car with the curious kitten in a crate on her lap, Frank put the car in gear. "Tomorrow. Meet here at ten in the morning. No excuses." He said the last sentence staring right at Vee. Then he rolled up the window, and the Toyota rolled out of the parking lot.

"Frank and Nadine hate us," Aneta said.

"The Cat Woman hates us," Esther said.

"The cats hate us," Sunny said.

"*Beetle!*" Vee said. And sprinted for home.

At ten the next morning, Nadine and Frank and the girls were already in the community center parking lot by the time Vee's dad pulled his big SUV alongside the Toyota. Dad hadn't been too happy about having to bring her all the way from his house this early. Thankfully, the Twin Terrors didn't clamor to come since they were watching *Everything Animal*, their favorite Saturday show.

Frank and Nadine pointed to the senior center door. "Here we go," Frank said, rubbing his hands together like a mad scientist. "Muahahaha!"

"Creepy," Sunny commented, but she started to smile.

"Are we still in trouble?" Aneta asked, following behind Sunny.

"You're not helping, Frank," Esther said, hands on hips, falling in. Vee shrugged and picked up the end.

Nadine took them to the room with the big-screen TV, turned out the lights, and started the video. While the narrator was explaining the concept of "trap, neuter, and return" as more helpful than simply exterminating the community cats, Vee took notes. At the end, she said, "You guys, I'm sorry I made such a mess of catching the cats. I just wanted to get it all done and get going so I could focus on my retest."

"Trapping," Esther said, "not catching. Cat Woman says." But she smiled quickly.

Sunny said it wasn't like Vee's brain was the only one that was supposed to work. "None of us thought this out. We just wanted to work together like we did last time."

"Last time was not good at first," came Aneta's voice. When the girls turned toward her, she was smiling with her head cocked and eyebrows raised. Sunny spluttered, clapping her hand over her mouth, Esther's eyes crinkled up as she held back laughter, and Vee snorted. Yeah right. Their beginning had not been fun.

"For pizza sakes, we've got to help those cats," said Sunny.

Top Things to Know about This Project:
   1. Not all community cats want to be pets.

2. *We could do a lot of work and not make any of them into pets.*
3. *We could fail our service-learning project.*

What about the retest? Vee licked dry lips. The weeks seemed suddenly very short. Could she keep her want-to ramped up to find her spot as the family smart kid? Find the curious kitten a spot? Find all the Dumpster cats a home? Could she do it *all*?

She sighed, thought of the curious kitten's sad little meow yesterday. Thought of Dad's less-than-happy reaction to the whole project. If only the project were more *important*. . . . Her brain began to buzz. Like if a *national TV show* filmed their wonderful Great Cat Caper Adoption Event? So what if that narrator guy sounded like community cats rarely became adoptable. Weren't they the S.A.V.E. Squad?

The girls were waiting.

"The"—she thought quickly—"Great Cat Caper Adoption Event!" She stood, held out her arm with the Squad bracelet on it. "It will be for the cats. Agreed?" *And bring the kitten home.* That sad little voice was getting louder. Vee pushed it away. And *Everything Animal* would be there. *That should make Dad proud.*

Three other bracelets joined hers until their fingers were intertwined.

"Agreed!" the girls chorused.

She would e-mail the show tonight. As soon as the answer came, she would tell the girls. She imagined their leaping and shrieking. Operation Catness was still a stellar plan.

Chapter 15

Cat Taming

By Monday, the girls had decided the mom cat would be Sunny's project, Aneta would take one of the adult cats, and Esther would work with the other adult cat. That left Vee the curious kitten—a male, they learned—and the second kitten the girls figured was the brother to the curious kitten. The two kittens seemed to do well in their trap together. Frank and Nadine had decided the cats would stay in an empty conference room at the Senior Center while the girls socialized them. When the Squad arrived, the Cat Room was already open.

The girls stood outside. "Frank told us we had to keep it closed for the people who have allergies," Vee said, frowning.

The shuffling steps of Hermann sounded, and the old man approached them. "Wild kots to pets," he said. "It vill never verk." He shuffled into a nearby room and slammed the door.

Vee sniffed. Medicine-y mouthwash. Weird. Now there was no one but the girls in the hall. Hermann didn't smell like mouthwash.

When Frank strolled down the hall a few minutes later, they made sure to tell him it had been open, but it wasn't their fault.

On Tuesday, the girls raced each other to the lake and back and then spent time reading to the cats in the sheet-covered cages. Esther brought books from the children's side of the library.

"All stories about cats who love people," she said, passing out the books. Sunny read in funny voices and made everyone laugh. At first Aneta didn't want to read until the other three got on their knees, clasped their hands, and begged her.

"You like people, you like people," Vee told the curious kitten behind the sheet. "So does your brother." The brother hissed. She wondered if Bill liked cats. She wondered about mouthwash and the box of rat poison by the senior center door. Fortunately, it was unopened, but why was it there? Frank was looking a little more serious about Vee's report of mouthwash.

"I think it's Hermann, trying to wreck our projects," Esther said.

"That would be mean. He would not do that," Aneta argued.

In the end, there was nothing left to talk about. Maybe these things were just mistakes.

That day, the moment Vee returned home from the cat training session, she headed for the family computer and checked her e-mail. None from *Everything Animal*. She finished her homework early, left Bill to his weird leftovers, and joined Heather and the Twin Terrors at Burger Mania. The Terrors bonded by sticking french fries in each other's ears and spilling orange drink. Vee bonded to the idea that she didn't want to do that again anytime soon.

On Wednesday, she checked her e-mail before leaving for school. Nothing. She survived learning how to reduce a fraction in math— again. After school, the first to arrive at the Cat Room, she surveyed the cages, smiling at the cats and in particular, at the curious kitten. Her smile died. The door to the curious kitten and brother cage was slightly ajar. Fortunately, the two kittens were sitting in the rear litter box, watching Vee.

Fastening the door as Esther arrived, Vee said, "Okay, I am not crazy, but this is the second time I've smelled super mouthwash and there's been something not right with the Cat Room." She told her about the door.

"You're imagining things," Esther said, going to her cat's cage and checking the door. "Mine's okay. Why would yours be special?"

Because the curious kitten was special?

After the other girls came, they sang silly songs to the cats. Puzzling over another strange occurrence, Vee trotted home and endured another session with Math Man.

On Thursday, she checked her e-mail before breakfast. Nothing from *Everything Animal*, and the days were melting away to the retest. At the senior center, Frank said they could take the sheets off, and they did. Momma Cat blinked. The two adult cats hissed and stayed in the farthest corner of their traps. Curious kitten and his brother sat side by side, twitching their tails in unison. The girls called it a great start. Vee wasn't so sure. Aneta's Gram and The Fam arrived on the brightly colored scooters they drove, placed a girl behind each driver, and headed to The Sweet Stuff. That night, Vee dreamed of the curious kitten swatting numbers as she held him.

Friday finally came. Operation Catness would escalate—picking up the cats and removing them from their cages.

Sunny bounded in. "I did some research online. Since Momma Cat used to be someone's cat, if she had a good experience with people, she might be faster turning back into a pet. Yayness!" She looked at the girls. Aneta's eyebrows shot up, and she clapped her hands.

"How do you know she was a pet?" Esther was skeptical.

"One of the ladies at the senior center thinks she remembers a family that moved from her street owning a cat like Momma Cat. We figure they left her behind. Ugh."

Nadine and Frank entered the room, arm in arm. Vee hoped the curious kitten would leap into her arms and start to purr. She grinned. She could hope, couldn't she?

Cocking her head, Nadine glanced over at Sunny, who was pulling something over her hands. She began to laugh. "Sunny, you nut. You're prepared. But, slowly, Sunny. Very slowly."

Vee frowned. What was Sunny doing? Those things on her hands looked like. . .oven mitts?

Sunny spun around, holding up her pumpkin-decorated oven mitts. "Yes! My mom got a pair for each of us at the dollar store."

On the table were three more pairs of oven mitts. Each girl took a set. Aneta slipped them on, holding them up like mittens. "Maybe I will try my cat today, too!"

Sunny began to dance around the chairs then, with a quick glance at the traps, made a *yikes* face and settled in the nearest chair.

"I want to go first," Vee said. "The curious kitten has been looking at me since we took the sheets off. Okay?"

"Sure," everyone chorused.

"Here goes." Vee approached her curious kitten and brother's cage. Very slowly and quietly. So far so good. No hissing. Sunny slid up the door, and Vee slid her mitted hands in. The brother skittered to the back, but the curious kitten remained on the blanket in the middle of the trap. He blinked at Vee. Vee blinked at him.

"Okay, kitten," she said. "I'm going to put these mitts on you and take you out."

Sunny giggled. Vee twitched.

Making a "sorry" face, Sunny whispered, "It just sounded funny to say 'put my mitts on you.' "

Now the mitts were on either side of the kitten. The brother kitten growled. The curious kitten's tail puffed up, and he darted backward, out of the mitts. Frank told Vee to back out. Crushed, she did as she was told. Sunny slid the door shut.

"Tomorrow," Frank said. "You can try again tomorrow. Esther, go ahead."

Esther approached her trap cage with her oven mitts in place. Sunny slid up the door. A growl that sounded more like a monster than a cat leaped out of the trap. Esther's face fell, and she jumped backward. The gray-striped cat inside opened his mouth as wide as it would go and displayed every tooth in his head. The gurgling grunt increased in volume. The cat's eyes were wide with the pupils narrowed to slits, whiskers flat against its head.

Creepy, thought Vee.

"Wow," Sunny said, sliding down the door. "Something that small can make a scary sound."

Esther looked at Frank. "What did I do wrong?"

"Nothing, Esther. It could be a stray, but if it was born in the wild, we can consider it *feral*, or wild."

Even though she nodded and returned to her seat, Esther's face looked like she was ready to cry. Vee knew that feeling. Esther was smart, and being smart meant you wanted to be smart in everything. Even cat taming.

Aneta's round face was pink with excitement as she approached her trap. But before Sunny could lift the door, the horrific growling and grunting began. Aneta stood with her mitted arms up, her lower lip quivering.

Momma Cat was at the front of her trap, tail wrapped around her, squinting and eyeing the group.

Frank's voice broke the people silence and interrupted the cat noise. "Sunny? You ready to try your Momma Cat?"

Hermann strolled through the door. "You kits should just give up." The Cat Woman glided in behind him and told him to be quiet. They must have some sort of cat radar, Vee decided.

Sunny donned her mitts. Nadine slowly raised the end of the trap. Momma Cat sat still, watching everything.

"Remember, slowly, Sunny," Nadine said. "If she begins to struggle, put her down, okay?"

Sunny nodded. "Help me help Momma Cat, Lord," she whispered and ever so slowly put her mitts in the cage. Momma Cat's whiskers shot forward, and her ears came up. Sunny reached the cat and carefully held her between the mitts, drawing her toward the open end of the cage.

"Um, God, it's Vee. Let Momma Cat know Sunny's okay." The words were out of Vee's mouth before she thought about it. The girls told her God created everything, so she figured He must know Momma Cat.

In another moment, Momma Cat was out of the cage and against Sunny's chest. The cat didn't exactly look happy, but not unhappy either.

Hermann creaked to his feet. "One kot. You vill never get dem all into pets." Shaking his head and muttering about crazy children, he left.

"Now what?" Sunny whispered. "I want to spin, but I don't want to scare her. I'm so excited!"

For a moment, nobody said a word. Momma Cat began to purr. Then a quiet whisper floated through the air: "Thank You, Lord." It was Sunny, her face shining.

It's Vee, again. Thanks, God. That was pretty cool. Vee looked at the curious kitten. Yep. It was watching her. *Next time, it's our turn.*

A light tap sounded on the door, and Aneta's grandmother entered. "Hey, girls. Is this a good time for The Sweet Shop?"

Is it ever.

Chapter 16

But, Dad!

Hey, Veelie." Dad called after supper while she and Bill were cleaning up from Mexican takeout. No baked potatoes. Yayness, as Sunny would say.

"Hey, Dad, the coolest thing happened today. With our project. Sunny's cat purred when she took it out of the trap. So tomorrow—my cat! I just know it."

"That's great, honey."

He didn't sound like he was paying attention.

"I've got a big favor to ask of you, honey," her dad said. "I need you to come this weekend—now—for our weekend instead of next weekend."

A rumble of angry words sounded in her head. "Why?"

"The boys won a soccer award, and our family needs to be together when they receive it."

Our family. That wasn't *our* family. That was *his* family.

"I can't, Dad. I just said that tomorrow is the day I'm sure the curious kitten will let me hold it. This is my school project."

She heard an impatient sound on the other end of the line. "Vee, your project is cats. Dumpster cats. I think your little brothers are more important."

"But, Dad, it's movie night here." Even though it would be just her and Bill tonight. Mom had already headed for bed after dinner. "*Our* family thing."

"Vee, how often do I ask you to do something for me?"

If she thought about it, she could come up with a list. But she was getting mad. "So if I come this weekend, I don't have to come next weekend?"

"Veelie, honey, you can come both weekends if your mother will let you. You know I always want to see you."

Especially if the soccer team needed somebody to hold jackets and cut oranges.

"Fine." She bit the words out. "When are you picking me up?"

A crash sounded in the background. Vee waited for him to yell at the Twin Terrors. Instead, unbelievably, Dad laughed. "Your brothers are so crazy," he said. "I'll be by in about forty-five minutes. Make sure you're ready. Wait for me out front, okay?"

"Anything you want, Dad." Vee punched off the phone. When she turned around, she realized Bill was standing there. He looked like a deer caught in headlights.

"I didn't know whether I should leave and be distracting or stay and be quiet," he said. "So you think your curious kitten will let you hold him?"

"I guess I won't find out till Monday now," Vee snapped. Bill's eyes widened. "I'm sorry, Bill. I can't be here for movie night tonight. I have to go pack." She stomped up the stairs, threw a few clothes in her gym bag, and stomped into her mother's room.

"Dad says I have to go this weekend because the Twin Terrors are getting some stupid award," she said to her mother's sleeping body and stomped out to the front steps. Belatedly, she thought about checking her e-mail, but a stomping exit meant she couldn't go back into the house. In fact, if her mother hadn't been asleep, she would have been busted on the stomping. Oh yes, this weekend was shaping up to be a real *beetle-y* one.

As usual, Dad's forty-five minutes was an hour. When his SUV pulled into the driveway, Vee stood. Her dad motioned from the window. "C'mon, Vee. We're taking the boys out to dinner to celebrate."

"I already ate." Vee crossed to the passenger side and opened the door, but didn't get in.

"What?" he said. "I thought we were done with this. You can sacrifice Dumpster cats for your brothers. They are part of your family now. Get in."

"I'm not getting in," she said and sucked in a breath. Her bravery or stupidity nearly paralyzed her.

Her dad flung his head back against the tall headrest. His tone, when he spoke, was like he was talking to a small, angry child. "Okay, Vee, what is it you want to talk about that is so important and has to be discussed"—his voice was increasing in volume—"*right now?*"

"I'll come this weekend," she said, standing straight. "And have a good attitude and smile all weekend."

"Where's the 'but'?" her father asked.

"I'll come, but you have to show up at the senior center at 3 p.m. on Monday to watch me work with the curious kitten and see our project. Meet Frank and Nadine. At least *act* interested."

Her dad sat quietly, staring out the front of the windshield. He turned to her, and his voice was warm like it used to be when she and he used to watch Saturday morning shows together. "Yes, Vee. I will come see your cat—"

"Kitten."

"Kitten. Monday at 3 p.m. in the senior center."

Vee climbed into the SUV and shut the door gently.

Chapter 17

Whaap Attack!

On Monday, Vee told herself to forget the previous weekend. Today was the day the curious kitten—and maybe his brother, too—would let Vee pick them up and take them out of the cage. Dad was coming to watch. That was all that was important.

"Hey, Squadders," she sang out. Esther, Aneta, and Sunny were clustered around Momma Cat who was sitting on the table, feet tucked underneath her body. Aneta had changed out of her school uniform into a knit shirt and capris and sandals. Vee wondered how late in the year she'd be wearing those sandals. Sunny had her usual T-shirt but had added a very ratty pair of jeans instead of the shorts she'd worn all summer. Esther had new nail polish—a different color on each finger—and was wearing long earrings that looked like they were made of feathers. Once she had joined them, Vee confirmed they were feathers. Turquoise feathers with beads.

Hermann walked in, carrying a tall carpeted pole with several shelves on it and a solid base. One section was wrapped in rope. "A kot needs a kot perch. I make it for you. I come to vatch you tame the kot." He set it in the corner.

Hermann made something for our project? Vee shot a look at the girls. They looked between the pole and Hermann and back again.

Sunny, of course, had to know. "Why are you nice to us all of a sudden?" she asked, folding her arms.

Hermann shuffled his feet, embarrassment all over his lined face. Glancing toward the door, he whispered, "Dot Cat Woman, she told me if I do not help you, she vould come to my house every day to cook my dinner." He shuddered. "Every day." Another low whisper. "My house. Every day dot voman vould come."

The girls, wide-eyed until the confession was finished, began to giggle. He drew himself up. "Every day she say. She vould, too. I can cook my own dinner." He settled into a chair, folded his arms, and acted like he wasn't a bit interested in what was going on.

No matter *how* Hermann had become the cats' friend, the cat perch would be a great addition as the cats grew tamer. Now they would have something to tell Mrs. Sissy when she asked—again—how much senior involvement the girls were receiving. Other than Hermann and the Cat Woman, not much. The girls didn't know why, although they had already put up signs asking for volunteers.

"Cool earrings," she said to Esther, to calm her own nervousness.

Esther grinned and shook her head. "I like how the feathers tickle my face. Watch." She bent her head forward and wagged her head back and forth.

Before Vee could notice whether they did, Momma Cat twitched her head toward Esther, shot out a paw, and snagged the feather.

"Ow!" Esther shrieked, leaning forward farther to prevent the earring from pulling.

"Momma Cat! Let it gooooo." Sunny gently took the cat's paw and disengaged the nails from the feather. Esther leaped back as soon as she was free. Momma Cat began to wash her face, but she kept an eye on those earrings.

Esther's face was crimson. Would it mean an explosion? Would

Esther decide to dump the project? Vee hurried to Momma Cat's defense.

"You know it was just the movement. I think she was—" She didn't get to finish because Esther was laughing. And laughing. And holding her stomach.

"Oh, you guys," she finally gasped. "That paw was so fast. Before I could jerk back, she'd grabbed it. It was like a blur!"

Through their laughter suspended, they heard a rusty, creaky sound like an old gate. It came from Hermann's direction. The old man was slapping his knee and chortling.

"Dot kot is de fastest kot I see!" he fell against the chair.

"Stop laughing," Vee ordered the girls fiercely, concerned Hermann might actually die laughing, but that only set them off again.

Sunny giggled. "It was a whapp attack," she said, her chuckles rolling to full-blown Sunny laughter.

More creaks and wheezing from Hermann.

Whapp attack sent Esther off again, this time with Aneta and Vee joining in. They laughed until Momma Cat got weirded out and looked like she might jump off the table. Then they pressed their hand over their mouths. Sunny stroked the cat to soothe her.

"Are we ready?" Vee nodded her head in the direction of the trap cages. "I know today's the day." *Where is Dad?* "You guys go first. My dad is coming, and I want him to see me take out the curious kitten."

It only took a few minutes for both Esther and Aneta to attempt and fail with their cats. The cats loudly proclaimed their refusal. Both girls got a little teary. Frank, who had arrived during Aneta's approach and denial, shook his head.

Vee kept an eye on the door and her watch. It was 3:20 p.m.

"Don't say it yet, Frank," Esther pleaded, a husky tone creeping into her voice. She sniffed. "I just have to keep trying."

The curious kitten and Vee regarded each other as Vee approached the cage. Dad wasn't coming. She would do this by herself.

"Mitts, doctor?" Sunny said, sounding like a nurse in the operating room. Vee held up her hands, and Sunny slid on the oven mitts.

"Mitts, doctor," she replied, her face serious.

"Approach the door, and Godspeed to you." Sunny stepped to the side and raised the door.

The curious kitten and his brother watched the oven mitts enter the trap cage. The brother hustled back to his place and hissed. The curious kitten came forward and sniffed the mitts, whiskers forward. Vee held her breath. The kitten took another step into the mitts.

Today is the day, today is the day, ran the joy in Vee's mind.

"Caaaats!" A human scream, as horrible as any of the cat shrieks, rolled into and around the room. Hermann fell off his chair. The curious kitten's eyes blazed wide, and he retreated. Desperately, she plunged the mitts farther in to catch him, and that set off the brother who hauled forth the most uncatlike screeches and yowls. Vee removed the mitts and turned. Aneta and Esther helped Hermann up.

"*Who* was that?" Vee cried, stamping her foot, pulling off the mitts, and throwing them on the table. The doorway was empty. Vee ran toward the door and peered both ways in the hall. Nobody. Nothing but the heavy smell of mouthwash.

"I'm telling you there's a woman who smells like mouthwash who. . ." Her voice trailed off. Who did what? Vee didn't have any proof.

Frank made the girls walk down to the lake and back before they all headed for home. When they came back, breathless, he said, "You girls can't take this so hard. It was probably someone who was upset about something else." He locked the Cat Room. Vee watched him carefully.

Aneta sighed. "I have been dreaming about my cat." Making a face, she sighed again. "He yowls in my dreams, too."

Hmph. In *Vee's* dreams, her Dad would actually show up.

Chapter 18

Super Bill to the Rescue

Why hadn't Dad shown up? Vee made it home with ten minutes to spare before Math Man darkened the door. She grabbed a stick of string cheese from the fridge and walked out through the breezeway to stick her head in Bill's garage and tell him she was home. She hoped tutoring went better than the cat work had. She was feeling pretty discouraged. The mayor was expecting something wonderful, and all they had was Momma Cat. It was a good thing *Everything Animal* had never responded. What would they film? Momma Cat whapping Esther's earrings? Vee talking about the mystery of the mouthwash lady?

Thinking of the show made her think of her e-mail, so she moved over to the computer on the rolling desk in the kitchen. While it booted, she poured a glass of grape juice and then sat in front of the computer. Why wouldn't the curious kitten be tamed? She'd pretty much given up on the brother. He had never ever been interested in the humans, other than to use them for developing his vocal cords.

She clicked into her e-mail, took a swallow of juice, and looked at her in-box. The next second, grape juice sprayed on the computer screen.

On the way home from school the next day, Vee ran. Ran as hard and as fast as she could. Everything was wrong. Math class was wrong. Dad was wrong, Mom working so much was wrong, the curious kitten was wrong, *Everything Animal*'s e-mail saying they were coming on *Friday* was wrong. *Wrong, wrong, wrong.* As she reached her house, thumped up the front steps, and inserted her key in the lock, she knew there could not *possibly* be a sixth-grade year that was *worse* than hers was turning out to be.

Lying in her bed after a peanut butter and honey sandwich and a string cheese, Vee stared at the swirls on her ceiling. Storm clouds. That's what they were. Or oven mitts chasing snarling kittens.

A light tap sounded on the door. *Go away.* She knew it had to be Bill. There had been yet another note from Mom on the kitchen island about an appointment. Pretty soon there wouldn't be any houses left for sale in Oakton. They'd have to move so Mom could work on the rest of the state of Oregon.

"Go away."

"Okay. Just checking," came the muffled voice on the other side of the door. " 'Cause if you *were* here, you wouldn't be at the senior center with the S.A.V.E. Squad taming cats."

The Squad! She had completely forgotten! How could she? Heavier and heavier pressed the weight. Math class, math tutoring, bonding with the Twin Terrors, Dad's not understanding and not showing up, the looming retest.

She flung herself back on the bed and began pounding her fists on the comforter. *"Beetle! Beetle! Beetle-y! BEEEEEEEEEETTTTTLLLLLLEEEE!* I'm just a sixth grader. I

CAN'T TAKE THIS ANYMORE!" It felt so good to pound her fists and yell that she began pounding her heels, too. The bed began to jiggle. "Too much, too much!" she said, shouting in beat to the jiggle of the bed. Dad should see her now. He would never want her to bond with the Twin Terrors.

Suddenly the door burst open, and Bill was in the room. Vee sat up. "You're not supposed to come in without—" The rest of what she had prepared to shout died on her lips. For Bill had leaped lightly to the end of her footboard. It creaked alarmingly. Bill shouted, "To the rescue, it's Soooooo-per Bill!"

"Super" Bill wore a bright orange pasta strainer on his head, a garbage bag cut open for his head and arms, and was brandishing long, long tongs he used when he barbecued. "She yells 'Beeeetle,' "—he howled out her interjection even better than she had, she thought admiringly, drawing her knees up to a cross-legged position to gape up at him. Bill seemed like Gulliver in the land of whoever those little people were—"and Super Bill comes to help." Continually trying to keep his balance on the narrow edge, he flailed his arms. "He—has the"—wobble, wobble, flail, flail—"Helmet of Hardiness so no insult from Go Away Girl can permeate him."

Permeate. Cool word. She'd have to look that one up. A bubble of giggle was beating through the ick, and any moment she just might laugh. Maybe. It had been a very long string of ick.

Gesturing to his garbage bag, Super Bill turned sideways to better balance himself. It wasn't much better. He still looked like he was going down. "And the Toga of Tears should she need to cry!" He wobbled mightily. "And the Tongs of Removal of all ick!" Then, with a wild yell, he fell backward off her bed.

A prickly sensation burned at the back of her eyes as she bounced to the end and peered over. "That's gotta hurt," she said.

"Yeah," Bill gasped, stiffly rolling to his side and then to a cross-legged position. He gushed out a breath. "So. Is the Go Away Girl going to meet her friends?"

Vee immediately retreated to the middle of her bed. "No."

She heard the groans and sighs as Bill crawled to the end of the bed. "Will the Go Away Girl tell Super Bill about the ick? He is prepared," he said, brandishing the tongs.

Humans were weird, Vee decided later after she had dumped Dad's desertion, the *Everything Animal* e-mail, how to tell the girls, and math in general on Super Bill. She donned the Helmet of Hardiness, cried on the Toga of Tears, and danced around poking the Tongs of Removal into pillows Bill provided. So weird. How could she cry and laugh at the same time and feel so much better?

Chapter 19

Cat Chaos

"Good day for treasure," Bill said the next morning as Vee clumped down the stairs, bleary eyed from dreaming of twin boys chasing her with numbers. Bill, predictable as ever. "You gonna talk to the girls today?"

Pouring herself a glass of milk and plopping two slices of rye bread into the toaster, Vee shuffled to the counter and struggled onto a stool. "Yeah." Even though she was sure the girls would forgive her, Vee didn't want to deal with the whole thing.

Fishing in his pocket, Bill drew out his wallet and removed a bill. "Super Bill, although he does not have his gear on this morning, would suggest you talk on neutral ground. Say, The Sweet Stuff?" He slid the bill toward Vee.

She slid it into her pocket, tears welling up. How had she ever thought Bill was just okay? He was the best. Stopping by the computer, she shot an e-mail to the girls about meeting at The Sweet Stuff. *Important stuff to tell you*, she typed.

In the sweet-smelling sanctuary of The Sweet Stuff, Vee made her apologies and told the girls about *Everything Animal*'s Friday visit. Their forgiveness came quickly and their reaction to the news that they would be on national TV more than satisfying. It was the only bright spot in the week, Vee thought, walking home with the girls.

Friday, *Everything Animal* day, arrived quickly. Sunny, Aneta, and Esther were standing outside the Cat Room's open door when Vee arrived out of breath after school. Their faces told her there was a story.

"What?" she asked.

"We should have told them not to come." Esther shook her head.

"Who thought they *would* come?" Sunny performed a slow twirl and sagged against the wall.

"The Fam *always* comes," Aneta said simply.

"What?" Then Vee heard the buzz of many voices in the room. She peered around the corner and stepped back with a gasp.

"Yep. My parents and my brothers," Sunny said.

"My mom and my brothers," Esther said.

"My mom, my gram and grand, Uncle Luke," Aneta counted on her fingers. "They left Wink home. My cousins are away at college."

"Oh." Esther waved her hand in front of Vee's nose. "And your mom, Bill, Heather, and the Twin Terrors."

The Twin Terrors? Rushing panic swallowed up the excitement of meeting a real-life TV producer. Would Momma Cat's trap fit two seven-year-old boys?

"What if the cats make those horrible noises?" Aneta asked.

"They have been quiet this week. Maybe today they'll surprise us all," Esther said.

"We might as well go in," Sunny said, motioning them in as though directing a jet plane. "The producer has already met our families. She might as well meet us."

Just to be sure, Vee sniffed quickly as she entered. The room looked and smelled normal. Good.

The moment they were through the door, the applause began. Baffled, the girls looked at each other.

"What did we do?" Aneta wanted to know.

The mayor, raspy voice even more pronounced since she was nearly shouting, laughed and said, "You're our Junior Event Planners with another terrific community project!"

Sunny spoke to Vee from the side of her mouth. "For pizza sake. Have you got a plan for more than the cats? I don't."

A nudge from Esther on the other side. "What if she asks us what the other ideas are?"

Vee didn't respond since she had seen Heather and the Twin Terrors and was waving. The seven-year-olds pointed to her, whooped, and barreled through the tables and chairs, knocking over a few.

She shushed them and used both hands to gesture *slow it down.* "Slow down, Turbo," she said to the one she was pretty sure was Joshua. He had reached her first and was pretending to box with her, darting in and out. She raised her head to Heather, imploring. Her stepmother was on her way, always calm and serene.

There was Frank, looking like he needed another sheet. Nadine stood next to him, shaking her head at the noise. The Cat Woman appeared at Vee's elbow. Leaning close to Vee, she whispered, "I wasn't too happy at first with you girls. Thought you were lightweights." She patted Vee's arm, and her wrinkled face glowed. "Isn't it great to see Hermann helping? Can't wait to see the other fun stuff you girls hatch up for the Great Cat Caper." Hermann sat in the corner, and when the two turned his way, he pretended to be very interested in his socks.

Neither can we, Vee thought. "It will be unbelievable." Vee didn't have to remind herself why *she'd* forgotten. It was spelled m-a-t-h. Shooting a look at the tall, skinny woman who had to be the producer because she was the only person not carrying a camera that Vee hadn't seen before, Vee saw her nod to the girls. They approached the woman.

The producer was easily as tall as Bill and skinny as the new tree in the front yard at home. A woman about the same age and a guy a little older carried big cameras on their shoulders and were moving around the room, up to the cat cages, around to the crowd, and now, to Vee's discomfort, right in her face. She blanched.

"Hello," she said, extending her hand to the producer. "I'm Vee Nguyen."

The tall woman smiled broadly and reached for her hand. "Oh, you're the one who e-mailed me about your great idea. I'm Ginger Padlow, one of the producers for *Everything Animal*. We're excited to be here."

"Uh, great."

After Vee had introduced Sunny, Aneta, and Esther, the producer called the camera people over. "We'll need an establishing shot of the room. That's a community touch for sure. Then"—she motioned to the girls—"what are you going to do with the cats?"

"We're socializing them," Esther said.

For once, Vee was glad that Esther was the first to speak. Everything was kind of spinning together: noise, Twin Terrors, cats, wondering if the curious kitten would let her pick him up.

"Great. Tell me what you girls did first."

Made a mess of things. Vee was sure *Everything Animal* didn't want to hear that.

"Okay, so we caught the cats—," she began.

Esther interrupted. "Trapped. The Cat—*Gladys* says since they are wild, we had to trap them."

Vee sighed. "Yes, Esther. We *trapped* the cats."

"Wrapped them in sheets to they can begin to de-stress," Sunny provided.

"The cats? Like burritos? What do you mean?" Ginger's carefully made-up face looked perplexed.

The girls took turns explaining. Every few moments, Vee would turn and look at the curious kitten. Each time, the kitten was either washing his face or sitting with his tail around him, yet he was always watching Vee. Vee smiled. She caught Mom's eye, and Mom looked over at the kitten and nudged Bill.

"We talked to them through the sheet and told them we love them. Then we took the sheets off and read stories and sang to them." Aneta's voice was low and sweet.

An *awwwww* rippled through the room.

Esther picked up the explanation. "Paws 'N' Claws Animal Buddies has a TNR program, which stands for Trap, Neuter, Return. The cats will be neutered, and the tip of one ear clipped while they are under anesthesia so people know they won't be reproducing. They also get shots."

"Great. Now let's see you work with the cats. Will I be able to hold one?" Nadine handed her Momma Cat. Ginger spied the oven mitts. "What are these for?"

"Safety measures," Esther said. The girls donned the mitts and held them up like surgeons ready to operate.

"Adorable," the producer raved.

The crowd chuckled.

Score one for Squad cuteness.

"This cat was wild?" Ginger asked, stroking Momma Cat, who obliged by purring. The producers heavy eyebrows shot upward. The camera people stepped closer. "She's a cuddle bug."

Vee sent a "hear that?" look toward the curious kitten. *See how nice it is to have people hold you and say you're wonderful?* He blinked. Vee noted the whiskers, which flattened back when the kitten was panicked, had sprung forward. That meant interested. Good.

Score two for Momma Cat. So far so good.

"One of the ladies of the senior center remembers a family who had a cat that looked a lot like her. They moved about a year ago." Cat Woman slid between Vee and Ginger. "They abandoned her or couldn't find her the day they moved. Happens all the time."

"Wow," Ginger said, lifting Momma Cat to her face and nuzzling her head. "She's such a cutie." Then, while she still held Momma Cat, she gestured to Esther and Aneta. "Okay, girls." Turning to the camera people, she added, "Get in as close as you can. I want to see the cats' expressions. How 'bout you each open the cage at the same time? It would look so cute to have all those oven mitts going into the cages at once."

Frank, Nadine, and Sunny moved into place to be the door openers. "I got a ba-ad feeling about this," Frank muttered to his wife. Vee did, too. They had never done this before. What if the flicking-tail brother upset the curious kitten?

"Okay, as soon as you get them out of the cages, turn and face the camera and smile, okay? We'll just keep rolling. Then I'll interview you girls, see what else is in store for the Great Cat Caper. Sound like a plan?"

No, it sounds like major crunching-beetle-drama. Vee wanted to shout, "We have no plan past the cats!" This time the Squad had gotten themselves in waaaay over their heads.

Ginger didn't wait for Vee to answer. She shooed the girls toward the cages.

"Yikes," Sunny murmured, taking her position as door lifter by Esther's cat.

"You might want to start praying," Frank said in a low voice to Aneta, acting as her door lifter.

"Nothing like a little pressure." Nadine smiled at Vee.

"Oven mitts ready?" Esther held up her mitts.

"Oven mitts ready!" Aneta answered with a smile.

Dear Lord, it's Vee again. Do You have time to help me? Vee nodded to Nadine who looked at Frank and Sunny. Simultaneously, they lifted up the doors.

Another murmur in the crowd, this time of amusement.

Oven mitts at the ready, each girl placed her hands inside the crate. Esther's cat, already at the back of the cage, widened its eyes and lashed its tail. In the next cage over, Aneta's cat emitted a piercing shriek, wiping away the buzz of conversation. Vee looked over at it, her mitted hands moving toward the curious kitten, the brother in the litter box in the back thrashing the dust.

Vee focused on the curious kitten. He sat motionless, eyes wide in the tufty-eared little face as its gaze flicked between the incoming mitts and Vee's face.

1. *Take out curious kitten.*
2. *Hold him, turn to the cameras.*
3. *Smile.*
4. *Name him (what??).*

She stopped.

"What's wrong?" Esther asked, next to her, valiantly trying to clutch the all-over gray cat with the three black feet who kept moving around the cage. "Keep going. The cameras are rolling."

Vee shook off the idea of actually bringing the kitten home. "Okay, curious kitten. Let's check this off our list for taming you." Vee placed the mitts on either side of the kitten and began to ever sooooo slooowwly draw him out.

Off to her right, two high-pitched boy voices hollered, "Go Vee the B! Grab your kitten first!"

At the sound of the boys' voices, several things happened at once. Vee jerked and squeezed the kitten. The kitten's wide pupils zipped into slits, and it dug its way out of the mitts and up Vee's arm, digging in for stability.

"OW!" she yelled, yanking her arms from the cage.

"He's out! He's out!" Esther shrieked, dropping to the floor and lunging in vain for her cat who had streaked out of the cage, hung in midair, and then dropped to the floor. He was immediately lost in the tables, chairs, and many pairs of moving feet.

"He's over there—no wait, that's the other one!" someone shouted.

"My cat! My cat is out!" Aneta wailed.

Ginger bellowed at her crew. "Keep filming; get both sides of the room!" In obeying, they got in each other's way and then somehow crashed down in a tangle of legs with the Twin Terrors who thought this was hilarious.

"Vee, watch out. The flick-tailed kitten!"

Vee, her left hand cupped over the curious kitten who was clawing his way up her bare right arm, gasped. She felt a second furry object dig itself into her waistband. A light weight with a sting of claws progressed up the front of her shirt. She hollered, "Esther! Help! The Flick Cat!"

and clapped her right arm—with the clinging curious kitten—toward her chest to stop the upward flight of the now-named Flick.

The pressure on him only caused him to dig deeper for better climbing power. He climbed her shirt like it was a ladder to the stars. She heard the deep, guttural growl, looked down, saw the bugged-out eyes. His lips curled back to show white kitten fangs. He was heading straight toward her face. *Had Frank taken them to get their shots yet? Is rabies like leprosy? Will I have to live on an island all by myself?*

In the next ragged breath, Flick was up over her face, a last dig into her scalp before launching off.

"Ouch!" Her voice was lost in the cacophony of cats, camera people, and leaping, lurching bystanders.

"There he goes! Stop him!" the mayor screamed, pushing past one chair and tripping over another one. She landed on the floor. "My ankle!" she began to wail, rocking forward to grab her ankle.

Vee whirled toward the chaos, managing with difficulty to get the curious kitten off her arm and contain it, squirming, once again between the mitts. It began to hiss. "I'm sorry, I'm sorry. It wasn't supposed to be like this!" She begged him to chill out. "Don't hiss, don't hiss. This is the day I hold you." Everything was going wrong. "You're messing up my to-do list. *Please.*"

Esther, Frank, the mayor, and Aneta were yelling directions nobody was listening to. The mayor was screaming. Sunny was screaming.

Esther: "Shut the door! Hurry! Shut the *door*, Aneta!"

Frank: "Quit screaming!"

Mayor: "I am *not* screaming!"

Frank: "I'm not talking to you!"

"Don't you dare lose them!" Ginger bellowed again. Suddenly the cats were out of the room with a line of pursuers. Human voices echoed in the hall.

"They went right!"

"No, left, left! I saw a tail!"

Ginger, the remaining person in the room, was holding Momma Cat and looking a little dazed. Vee looked at her.

"I think we might have caused a bit of a furor," Ginger said, stroking Momma Cat like she was the only link to sanity.

Fur-or. Sounded like catness. "I would say yes," Vee replied, then blinked, looked down at the mitts, and up again. A delighted smile stole across her face. A curious buzz had begun in the mitts.

"What's that kitten's name?" Ginger asked, shifting Momma Cat to her other arm.

Name? Buried in the oversized oven mitts, the curious kitten looked like a striped head, black nose smudge with no body. He looked up at Vee and she down at him for a long moment. The mitts continued to buzz with the purring kitten.

"Buzz. His name is Buzz."

Chapter 20

We're Toast

*A*fter the *Everything Animal* cameras had captured the drama of the runaway cats and the tears of Esther and Aneta, the families headed home and tables and chairs were righted in the Cat Room. The producer insisted the girls sit in a semicircle where she kept repeating what "great entertainment" the escapade had provided the fans of the *Everything Animal* program. It wasn't a great time for Esther and Aneta. Vee's heart hurt for her two friends sitting on either side of her. Esther's face was streaked with tears, the same sort of tears that trickled down Aneta's cheeks.

Esther and Aneta's moms had not been too happy to leave the girls to an interview after their projects had jetted out the door; however, the two girls insisted that they "could deal" and wanted to finish what they started.

Ginger, who seemed to be reluctant to give Momma Cat to Sunny to hold during the interview, settled in her chair. "Esther and Aneta, your projects left the building. What's the next step?" Ginger asked, crossing one long, skinny leg over the other. The camera people stepped closer to the girls.

The next step, Vee thought, was that she was going to jump up and slug the producer. Poor Esther and Aneta.

Esther sat up straighter. "Now we learn how to make a managed cat colony," she said crisply.

Yeah, you tell her, Esther! Esther sounded just like the Cat Woman. Which was a good thing. The Cat Woman knew her stuff.

Before Ginger could ask another *your-heart-is-broken-how-does-it-feel* question, Esther turned to the nearest camera. "We'll make cat condos for the three cats that escaped and for the one that got away the day we trapped the others."

That's a S.A.V.E. Squad girl. Push her and she bounces back! Vee hitched in her chair, waking up the sleeping Buzz between the mitts. Wait until she told Mom and Bill about *this*.

Ginger goggled at Esther a tiny bit before recovering. Turning to Aneta, she asked, "What about you, Aneta? It must have been heartbreaking to watch the cat you'd worked with for, what was it—several weeks?—escape and disappear."

Burger Mania, the Twin Terrors, orange drink, and french fries. She'd lock Ginger in. For several hours. Maybe turn out the lights. That would serve Ginger right for making Aneta's face flush and her eyes fill with tears.

Aneta looked Ginger straight in the eye. "Yes," she said simply, a single tear tracking down her cheek. Then she explained about the S.A.V.E. Squad. "That is what a Squadder does."

Ginger signaled the camera people to stop filming. She shook her head with a smile that was both sad and pleased. "Aneta, you answered the tough interview question with a heart blaster and shut me down cold."

"I am sorry," Aneta said, alarmed. "I did not mean to be rude."

Waving a dismissive hand, the producer rose and stepped over to scratch Momma Cat under the chin. "You weren't. You girls were just being yourselves. The world better watch out with the S.A.V.E. Squad on the loose."

After the camera people cleaned up and they were headed out the door, Ginger stopped and regarded the girls. "I can't wait to come back. Who knows the spectacular things you'll come up with for the festival in a week?" Then she and her crew were out the door. Vee heard Frank and Nadine coming down the hall toward the Cat Room to lock it up.

"Who does know?" Aneta said, innocently, turning to Esther.

"Not us, we're toast," Esther said.

"Burnt toast," Sunny added.

"Without butter," Vee finished gloomily.

The three girls turned toward her. "Without *butter*?"

Vee squirmed onto a kitchen stool and dropped her head onto her hands. She couldn't believe the past couple of hours at the Cat Room. "Did all that really happen?" she asked Bill.

Bill was taking baked potatoes out of the oven. After all this stuff was over, she was going to have to show Bill how to cook something else, like maybe chicken, zucchini, and rice.

"It sure did." Bill tossed the hot potatoes up and down making little "ooo, ooo, ooh" sounds as he carried them to the granite counter. "So, what's up now? Your face is showing."

"Ha, ha," Vee replied. "Not only did we have the mess of losing all the cats except Buzz and Momma Cat, but the S.A.V.E. Squad needs an emergency sleepover to get ideas for the Great Cat Caper."

"Which is bad, why?"

"It's a prodigiously bad weekend for me."

"Since *prodigiously* came before *bad*, I am assuming it's a double bad?"

"Yeah."

"Be*cause*," he dragged out the word, "it's a Dad weekend?"

She nodded. Sometimes Bill noticed way more than she thought he did.

He leaned on the counter and waggled his eyebrows. "Then why don't you ask your dad if you can have the sleepover at his house?"

A-a-a-a-nd then other times he didn't notice *anything*. "Are you nuts? It's *prodigiously* complicated to be *me*. You want me to expose my friends to both families?" She leaned forward, eyes intense. "You *do* know the Twin Terrors live with my dad."

A broad Bill smile. He stood up to pull objects out of the refrigerator that only he would add to a potato while Vee considered his suggestion. The Squad had a week before Ginger and the *Everything Animal* crew returned with more cameras. Right now they had Buzz's story as a former Dumpster cat turned pet. She hunched her shoulders. Even though the Cat Woman would tend him and Momma Cat at the Cat Room as she did every weekend, Vee already missed him terribly.

"Bill, how do you feel about cats?"

Problems to solve:
1. *Where to have the sleepover*
2. *Come up with "spectacular" ideas for the Great Cat Caper*
3. *Bring Buzz home to his beanbag spot*

"So have the sleepover at one of the other girls' houses."

"I can't. Not since I pitched a fit that Dad forgot to show up for my project. If I don't go to Dad's on a Dad Weekend. . ." She swallowed the rest of the phrase. *I can't say Dad doesn't spend time with me.* She sighed. "Bill, it's not fun when you're right." She slid off the stool and headed toward the phone.

Chapter 21

Math Means Something?

Heather would be delighted. So delighted they would spend Friday night *and* Saturday night. Vee was embarrassed at Heather's reaction when the four girls arrived at Dad's house. Her stepmother came to meet them with outstretched hands and a broad smile. "I'm so happy to meet Vee's friends!" she said. She hugged each of the girls, hesitated, and then hugged Vee, who endured it.

"So where are Joshua and Jacob?" Sunny asked, pulling a small bag from her duffel. "My brothers sent them a present, to put up with us."

Wow. Sunny remembered the Twin Terrors' names? And brought them a *present* to put up with *them*? As Heather's smile grew wider, she called the two boys. No need to wonder where they were coming from. Pounding overhead and then thudding down the stairs, the twins launched themselves at Vee.

"Vee the B!" they yelled in unison, throwing their arms around her waist. With their weight against her, she lost her balance and down she went. Sigh.

"Hi, boys. Now get off me and go away." The girls helped pull the boys off Vee as they had begun wrestling over who would help Vee up.

Heather shook her head. "They love Vee so much."

For a tackling dummy.

"My brothers are the same with me," Esther said. "They drive me crazy, but I wouldn't want any other brothers."

"Yeah," Sunny chimed in. "Just about the time I want to tell Mom to give them away—again—they do something like *this*." She handed the bag to the one Vee thought was Jacob. The part in his hair seemed a little farther over than the one in Joshua's hair. Joshua snatched it, and a tussle ensued. The bag ripped open, and a fluorescent pile of fruit-smelling gummi worms spilled into the entryway. Vee groaned. It was going to be a long night.

Jacob pointed to Sunny. "She can stay."

Joshua pointed at Aneta. "She can stay 'cause she's pretty."

They both pointed at Esther. "She has brothers. She's cool."

"So glad we have your permission," Vee said.

Heather sent the boys off to play outside. "I know what you mean," she said, tucking her blond hair behind her ears. "I grew up as the only girl with six brothers. I adore them, but not every moment."

Vee's mouth dropped open. Nobody had told her Heather was a survivor. Heather laughed at her expression. "We need some more bonding time, Vee. I can tell you lots of ways to handle these guys. You know why they call you Vee the B?"

"Because they don't know many words?"

Heather laughed so hard that she had to lean against the wall. She shooed the girls into the family room that opened out onto the backyard. She indicated where they could stash their sleeping bags, pillows, stuffed animals, backpacks, and drawstring bags. "No, although they do admire that *you* know so many. Jacob wants to bring you to class for show and tell. Joshua came up with 'Vee the B.' It stands for Vee the Best."

"Awww," Sunny said, nudging her. "The Twin Terrors have a heart."

The girls settled their bags, got the promise from Heather that the Terrors would not be joining them, and kicked off their shoes.

"When's Dad coming home?" Vee asked Heather as her stepmother passed through with a load of folded clothes.

"Probably by six thirty, usually," Heather said, cocking her head to think. "Unless, of course, he doesn't."

"Yeah, I know that deal."

Heather pointed to a pad of paper by the phone. "I've already called Pizza Crazy. They know to make whatever you want, and they will deliver. I've already taken care of the tip for the driver. Fruit juice in the door of the fridge. Ice cream in the freezer. The family room is yours." She moved away. Vee placed a hand on her arm.

She really wants us here. Given them their own spot. The Twin Terrors, in their sticky, bumpy way had made a spot for her. True, it was usually on the floor when they greeted her, but still. "Thanks, Heather."

Her stepmother blushed. "I'm so glad you're here."

"Go ahead," Vee said, opening her arms. "I know you want to."

Heather squeezed her in a quick hug and left.

Rejoining the girls, Vee clasped her hands in her lap. "Okay. Pizza now or after some brainstorming?"

"I say pizza now," Sunny said. "Pizza helps me think."

In customary fashion, they argued over what pizza to get and finally agreed on two large pizzas, one with half everything (Sunny) and half cheese (Vee) and one with half veggies and no meat (Aneta) and half Canadian bacon and pineapple (Esther).

After Vee handed out paper and pens—watching Esther out of the corner of her eye to see if the girl would roll her eyes—she did—the girls began throwing out ideas.

Hours later they had eaten both pizzas, talked about whether Melissa Dayton-Snipp would ever return to Oakton, relived the chaos at the Cat Room and the utter coolness of Buzz becoming tame—and that Sunny's uncle was relocating his horse ranch to Oakton and he'd promised Sunny her friends would get to ride horses. They'd argued over whether the Twin Terrors were more obnoxious than Esther and Sunny's little brothers (no way, Sunny and Esther insisted) and agreed that Aneta's family was the most crazy-fun. They went over every fun tidbit of their first adventure together, how they met, and laughed till they lay on the floor, sides heaving.

Esther was the first to recall their purpose for the sleepover. "Guys, we have to get to work."

"So we keep freaking out that we don't have anything," Sunny said, shifting onto her side and propping her head up with her right arm. "What if we write down what we do know so far? A wild list." The girls began to chatter; Vee had to scribble messily to keep up.

A Wild List
We, the S.A.V.E. Squad, do hereby know this:
1. *We are saving cats.*
2. *Buzz is the best former Dumpster cat (that was Vee's).*
3. *Cats eat.*
4. *Cats use a litter box.*
5. *Cats like Esther's earrings.*
6. *Cats have really cool eyes and whiskers.*
7. *Adoptable cats like to be petted.*
8. *We want great people to adopt great cats.*

The girls read over Vee's shoulder where she sat cross-legged on the floor. Sunny jumped up and did a little dance. "Nice job, Vee!" she said, collapsing back next to the girls. "We all talked at once, and you got a list."

"But what good is it?" Vee stared at the list. It was so random. You couldn't make events from stuff like this.

"I like the Buzz part," Aneta said thoughtfully. "Do you think your mom and dad would let you adopt Buzz?"

Vee had been trying not to think about that all evening. His little tufty face showed up in her mind.

"There are patterns," Esther said suddenly. "Connections, as my math teacher says."

Eww. Why ruin a fun time with math? Vee wrinkled her nose. "Where?"

The stocky girl moved to her hands and knees and lifted one arm to point at Vee's list. "See? Take 'cats eat' for starters. What do cats eat?"

"Food," Vee said. "I don't get it."

"Keep going." Esther didn't appear rattled with Vee's dismissal.

"Cat food," Aneta said, her brow furrowed. "And. . ." Her brow cleared. "Cat treats!"

Throwing up her arms like a referee indicating a touchdown, Esther beamed. "Right! So if we are *saving cats* and *cats eat*,"—she plucked the pen out of Vee's hand, apologizing as she did so—"what can we sell at the Great Cat Caper that's special?"

Aneta clapped her hands together. "Cat treats! We can make cat treats!"

Remembering Aneta's two experiences with cooking, Vee wasn't so sure, but Esther was. "Yes! There's our first activity. But, Aneta, remember you need someone to help you 'cause you're not so great yet with cooking."

"The Fam will help me," Aneta said with confidence, settling back happily. Vee knew they would. The Fam never missed one of Aneta's activities. *Must be nice. No,* she told herself sternly. *Dad apologized; drop it.*

"I'll go next," Esther said, moving the pen down until it came across the bit about cats and Esther's earrings. "If Momma Cat was drawn to my earrings, what if we make cat toys that dangle and maybe some with feathers? We can sell them."

"And give everyone who adopts a cat a cat toy!" Sunny snapped her fingers. "Esther, you're brilliant."

Vee thought she got it. Her eyes scanned the list. Cats eat, use a litter box, like to play with dangling things, and we want to save cats. Pattern: what a cat needs if they are saved. She began tentatively. "If they adopt a cat, we give them a. . ." Ideas began to jolt around her brain. "Cat Kit or Kitty Kit. It will have a cute litter box—"

"Are there cute litter boxes?" wondered Esther.

"Ours will be!" Sunny said, shushing her.

"And litter to get started—the kind Cat Woman said, nonclumping, whatever that is." Vee felt a thrill run through her. Patterns! Connections! This was like *math*? She wished she had Esther's math teacher.

"Oh, I get it!" Sunny was spinning again, this time around the family room. "The Cat Kit will also include a cat toy and a cat treat."

"And then we can sell the Cat Kit to people who want to give it to people as a present or for themselves!" Esther was with it now, writing down what each of them had said as quickly as she could. "My math teacher will freak when she hears our patterns and connections." She paused, pen in midair. "I wonder if she'll give me extra credit?"

"Oh, yayness! They can buy the Cat Kit and donate it to Paws 'N' Claws or the city animal shelter!" Sunny said.

The girls fell backward. Vee thought of Buzz. *I'm buying him a Cat Kit. I hope it comes with him to my house to live!*

"I need a drink after all that work," Sunny said.

The girls trooped into the kitchen and put vanilla ice cream into tall glasses of orange juice.

"Yum," Sunny said.

As they sat around the table, Vee dashed back for the list. "Okay, so we've got a few things left."

"Read what's left," Esther ordered, pointing at Vee with a drippy straw.

What's left:
1. *Cats have really cool eyes and whiskers.*
2. *Adoptable cats like to be petted.*
3. *We want great people to adopt great cats.*

"Easy, peasy," Sunny said, after sucking up the very last drop from what she named a Van-orange Float. "A Petting Palace."

"Palace?" Aneta wasn't sure of the word.

"A decorated place where a volunteer sits and lets other people pet the cats. Paws 'N' Claws Animal buddies will bring over their adoptable cats. We'll put them on princess pillows."

"The people?" Aneta still looked confused.

The girls busted out laughing.

"No, the cats will be on princess pillows. They'll all be washed and brushed. We'll get them neato-ba-deeto collars." Sunny was up and pacing.

"Neeto-ba-deeto?" Now Aneta was really lost. She sat back in her chair.

"Where?" Esther was practical.

"In the Cat Room, of course." Sunny's gaze searched the ceiling. "It will be magnificent."

If people were able to sit and love on the cats, they might think about what it would mean to adopt one. Vee already knew! "Wait!" She held up her hand. "Remember how much trouble we got into because we didn't learn about what it took to tame Dumpster cats?"

The other girls nodded.

"So maybe we should do something so people who come to the Great Cat Caper learn how to take care of cats before they adopt one."

"Yeah," Sunny said. "They won't have the Cat Woman or Frank and Nadine like we did."

Esther shot her hand in the air. "That's me! I can do a PowerPoint that's really cool. As Computer Coordinator, I learned how to do all that stuff. Plus I'll write a brochure." She shot a look at Vee. "Unless you want to write it?"

"No way, that would be great," Vee said.

"I'll take pictures," Sunny said, dumping over her empty glass. "The camera Uncle Dave gave me! Oh, yayness and oh, the catness of cats."

Vee heard a rustling, slithering sound from the family room. A moment later, two raspy voices hissed from the doorway. "You should paint cats!" Then the twins scurried away, snickering and snorting.

"They are so weird," Vee said by way of apology. She yawned and looked at the kitchen clock. Nearly midnight.

"No, very good." Aneta shook her head. "We will paint cat faces on people at the Helpful City Festival. That will make people ask them, 'Why is your face painted?' And they will say, 'We want to help save cats.' " She leaned back and skittered her gaze from Sunny to Esther to Vee.

"Yayness," Sunny agreed, yawning.

"It could happen." Esther covered a gigantic yawn.

"What you said," Vee said, leading the way to their sleeping bags.

As she fell asleep listening to Sunny, Aneta, and Esther say their prayers together and ask God to bless just about everyone on the planet, Vee envied them their spot. God seemed to like them. Sunday, as soon as she got home, she'd start in on Bill and Mom about Buzz and his spot. She fell asleep with a smile, seeing striped gray kittens with big eyes, black nose smudges, and tufty ears dancing around wearing oven mitts.

Chapter 22

From Spot to Place

Saturday, Heather took the girls to a movie the Twin Terrors disdained as a "girl movie." Then it was piles of spaghetti for dinner and playing soccer in the backyard with Dad and the Twin Terrors, who unbelievably behaved themselves and did not kick a ball into anyone's head.

The next morning, after Mrs. Martin picked up Sunny, Aneta, and Esther to return them home, Vee ducked into the shower before the Twin Terrors could submerge it with water, dressed, and headed to the kitchen where Heather was removing a breakfast casserole. It was their Sunday tradition. It smelled heavenly—Vee grinned at her Sunday comparison—and it was devoured quickly. Then they were on their way to church.

Usually when Vee attended church with her dad and his family, she dozed off and awoke only when the minister said a word more loudly than the rest of his words. Today, however, the music was upbeat and she found herself clapping along.

The Twin Terrors departed for Sunday school. Heather offered Vee the sixth-grade class, but she shook her head. Walk into a room where everyone would look at her? No thanks. So she sat between Dad and Heather's citrusy perfume and got comfortable, notebook and pen at the ready. Great thinking time for a plan to convince Mom and Bill that Buzz needed a spot, and Vee needed a spot, and the kitten and the girl could have their spot together in Bill's house. Technically, *Mom* and Bill's house. Neither of those sounded right anymore. Our house? She tried on the phrase as the minister began his sermon.

Our house. Wow. She forgot her list and stared ahead unseeing. It fit. When had it become our house? Mom worked too much, Bill was a bad cook and a nut case, and Vee—Vee knew what stuff had been going on inside her. Yet. *Our* house.

"Today is a great day for treasure." The minister's words finally penetrated Vee's thoughts. She glanced up. The guy sounded like Bill's every morning greeting. Were they related? No, this guy was short and bald. "Today's treasure is brought to you courtesy of the sixth-grade Sunday school class."

Vee counted a dozen kids her age who stepped up onto the stage. Eight stood in a line. The other four stood behind them. All of them carried cardboard squares with lettering. A murmur and a chuckle ran through the congregation. A boy with bangs covering his eyes stepped in front.

"So," he said, his face flushing scarlet. "We wanted to explain why God is our Treasure—kid school—not, like, adult old school. So, like first, we had to get ideas. Then we argued 'cause none of us had the same ideas and nobody would agree."

This provoked an outright chuckle in the room. Vee leaned forward, smiling. They sounded like the S.A.V.E. Squad.

"So we had to think what was more important, who had the ideas or getting good stuff for explaining treasure." He bobbed his head. "Dude, here we go. Hope it works."

The first person in line held up a sign. A kid popped out below and held out the explanation of the letter. Moments later, Vee was scribbling madly in her notebook, lifting her head up and down to keep up with the demonstration. The last kid had to dart after more letters than the others to finish the acrostic. He grinned at the audience as he popped in and out. They laughed. So did Vee as she scrawled the letters to the side in big print and the ideas next to it.

> *T ruth is, dude, life*
> *R equires*
> *E veryone to have*
> *A special spot*
> *S afe*
> *U nder God's Love,*
> *R egardless of*
> *E veryday trouble*

Treasure. She was sure she'd seen it in Buzz from the first time she saw him walking the Dumpster. When she'd named him, he'd become her treasure. She chewed the inside of her lip as the last song was sung. Her *special spot*. Hadn't she been looking for that ever since her parents married other people?

She thought of the connections and patterns the Squad had used to come up with kickin' ideas for the Great Cat Caper. Now her brain was clicking with a new pattern. What if *God could be the special spot. . .?* That kid with the long bangs would be able to tell her if she was right. As soon as the minister dismissed the congregation, she climbed over Dad's knees and marched up to the boy.

Chapter 23

C. P.?

"We've still got a lot to do," Vee said Monday after school when the girls gathered at The Sweet Stuff. The Helpful City Festival started Friday. And the retest. Gulp. Early Friday morning.

Aneta's gram had given her money for The Sweet Stuff. Everybody wanted to give them money. Her gram probably didn't know how often the girls had been to The Sweet Stuff lately. *Not for me to tell*, she thought with a grin, licking her cone.

To Do:
1. *Community cat shelters*
2. *Cat toys*
3. *Ask Mom and Bill to adopt Buzz*
4. *Cute litter boxes*
5. *Petting Palace*
6. *Ask Mom and Bill to adopt Buzz*

While they ate ice cream cones, Vee talked excitedly about the long-bangs boy, the treasure bit from yesterday, and how weird it was to be thinking now of God as treasure, her special place in Him, and wanting to see treasure around her. Sunny, Esther, and Aneta didn't think it was weird. That's why they were all the S.A.V.E. Squad, Vee thought with satisfaction. They thought alike even when they didn't.

She then handed out the list. Since yesterday, she'd been feeling, umm, *lighter*. When Bill greeted her with his morning greeting, she'd responded, "I found treasure yesterday." Bill wanted to know all about it. Funny. Bill knew all about God as treasure. Vee had shaken her head. You just never knew what Bill knew.

The Great Cat Caper would be the best ever. She couldn't wait to hold Buzz. While the girls were making their cat toys, she was going to get ideas from them about how to talk to Mom and Bill about adopting Buzz.

Esther poked her copy with one scarlet fingernail. "Couldn't we just once not have a list?"

Vee ignored her. "You've got the stuff for the cat toys, Esther? We're doing that tomorrow, right?"

"Check. I gave my list to Frank and Sunny," she nodded at the redhead. "And they are going around to the stores and seeing who will donate the stuff or money." Ticking off the items, she said, "Fake feathers, yarn, catnip, beads, and straws."

"Straws?" Aneta asked, pausing in midlick of her banana ice cream.

"You'll see," Esther said, smiling a secret smile. "Then Wednesday, we work on the cat colony shelters. My dad knows a guy who will donate two really big foam coolers."

"I don't see how cats can live in a cooler that's supposed to keep stuff cold." Vee frowned.

Again Esther smiled the secret smile and said, "You'll see."

Sunny, who could finish an ice cream cone faster than anyone Vee knew, was pacing around their table making up a song about cats.

It was pretty random.

A body rocketed into her vacant seat. "I gotta be in your group." It was C. P., looking desperate.

"You can't be in our group," Esther said patiently and not startled by his sudden appearance. She took another lick.

"Why not?" He pleated a napkin and pressed it to his upper lip. "See my mustache?"

"For one thing," Vee explained, trying not to laugh, "you're not a girl, and for another thing, you're not a S.A.V.E. Squad member."

He wiggled the mustache. "I don't want to be part of the creepy S.A.V.E. Squad. Cheez-Whiz, guys don't want to be in the S.A.V.E. Squad. I have to be in on the Great Cat Caper."

"Why?" Aneta fixed her wide-eyed gaze on him.

"Because if I don't find something else to do, my mom said she was going to lose her mind."

Sunny cocked her head. "But you play fall soccer."

"It's not in the budget this year."

Good day for treasure. What treasure might C. P. prove to be? What treasure might he be for the cats? *What on earth am I thinking?* It felt right, however, so she went with it. "I say yes," she said. "If nothing else, he can stir the organic cat treats, which are sure to be gross."

The other girls looked surprised but quickly added their okay.

"I knew you would," he said smugly then checked out Vee's dripping cone. "You gonna eat all that?"

Chapter 24

Freakies & Sock 'Ems

As soon as the girls and C. P. hit the senior center steps the next day, breathless from a race across the park—Vee won—Esther took charge. "Okay, let's see how many toys we can make before we have to go home."

"How many do we have to make?" Aneta wanted to know.

"You don't want to know," was Sunny's reply. "You should see all the stuff we got."

Sure as there were beetles, they needed help. Vee reviewed what she had to do today: An hour and a half of making a bazillion cat toys. Then Math Man's homework. Then regular homework. Vee just wanted to take Buzz home with his oven mitts, eat dinner with Mom and Bill, and play with Buzz until she went to bed. The math retest—and the key to whether she would get to stay in the Accelerated Learning Center—was three days away, counting today. The same morning the Helpful City Festival began. Dad was supposed to drive her to school for the test.

Esther was the first to turn the corner into the Cat Room. "Oh!" Vee heard her say.

"What?" Vee asked. She sniffed. No smell of mouthwash.

By now they had all stumbled into the room and saw Cat Woman, Hermann, an enormous man, and some ladies that played pickleball at the community center.

"We're here to help!" one of the ladies said.

"Hooray!" Sunny said.

"Hermann convinced us you girls really wanted help." Another lady unzipped her jacket and laid it neatly across the back of a chair.

The girls looked at each other. "We put up signs. We do need help!" Esther said.

"We signed up, but nobody contacted us."

Esther looked at Sunny. "Did you collect the sign-up sheets?"

"No," Sunny said. "I thought that was your job."

Oh boy. The S.A.V.E. Squad had done it again. This project had more messes in it than a Twin Terror birthday party. Vee and the girls traded glances.

"We're sorry!" Sunny said. "Boy, we sure are saying that a lot."

The ladies laughed and said it was nice to know someone else didn't remember everything. Vee got Buzz out of his cage and sat at the edge of the group, rubbing him on the belly and listening to his buzzing. Esther was organized, Vee was glad to see. If she hadn't been, C. P. could never have sat still long enough to get directions. As it was, he bounced up and down in his seat. Everyone got directions for the two projects.

Feather Freakies
List of supplies:
Fake feathers or bits from boas (let the birds keep theirs)
Straws
Scissors

Yarn

A medium to large bead for each Freakie

Steps:

Select three feathers.

Cut a straw in half.

Tie yarn around the tops of the feathers. Knot tightly. Leave long strings of the yarn to thread through the straw. Slide a bead over the yarn to the top of the straw. Tie those two ends to a piece of yarn long enough to dangle the Feather Freaky in front of the cat without getting your fingers grabbed. Your cat will freak. Keep it out of reach or the Freakie will have a short life.

Sock 'Ems

List of Supplies:

Baby socks, old or new from the dollar store

Yarn (bet you have some leftover from the Freakies)

Catnip (Paws 'N' Claws Animal Buddies sells it as a fundraiser by the bag.)

Steps:

Put a quarter-sized bunch of catnip in the toe of the baby sock (aren't they so cute and little?).

Wrap yarn tightly around the top of the sock and tie the knot there. Leave one or two long strings to diddle in front of the cat. They like it when you bump their face with it.

Added note: You can write the cat's name in a permanent marker on the sock before you fill it with catnip if you have more than one cat. Maybe they don't like to share.

By the end of their time together that afternoon, Vee knew that C. P.'s treasure was making them laugh. Her sides hurt from laughing.

"You, young man, are a card," one of the pickleball club ladies said. "You made my day. I can't wait to e-mail my granddaughter and tell her I spent the afternoon making Feather Freakies for the Great Cat Caper with kids. She thinks I never do anything but watch TV and eat Jell-O with my old friends."

"You are so funny," Aneta agreed, gathering the remaining feathers and neatly stowing them in a plastic bag.

Vee collected the beads and wound up the yarn. Tickling Buzz with one of the Freakies, she saw his eyes blaze and he pounced, fighting furiously with the feather and biting the straw. She giggled. "This toy is cat tested and passes with flying colors," she announced. Everybody clapped. She gently placed him in his cage.

Sunny began sliding the straws in another bag.

Esther finished counting. "We made 150 Freakies and 100 Sock 'Ems. We really sped up after C. P. said to cut all the straws and yarn first and measure out the catnip. And because we had help." She beamed at the seniors. The girls clapped.

Vee slung on her backpack after casting a quick eye around the table in the Cat Room. She hated leaving Buzz. "Bye, little Buzz. Tonight, no matter what, I'll talk to Mom and Bill. Or Bill, if Mom is working late."

Esther's voice followed her out the door, along with Sunny and Aneta's good-bye. "Remember, tomorrow we make cat colony shelters for Aneta's and my cats!"

Chapter 25

The Joy of Catness

$\mathcal{N}$ow Vee knew what a cat condo looked like. At least for community cats. The next day, two oversized foam coolers were taped shut and a circle cut for an entrance. Then the entire cooler was wrapped in wide, outdoor tape.

Cat Woman walked into the parking lot as they emerged from the senior center, headed toward the bushes where Vee had met Buzz and collected a face full of scratches. "Nice job, girls!" she called.

C. P. had insisted on carrying one by himself and had the girls whooping by staggering back and forth, trying to see over and around the shelter. Holding her end of the white shelter with Esther on the other, Vee smiled as the older woman joined them.

"Those two shelters should be great shelters for the three that escaped and the one that got away the day we tried to trap them," Cat Woman said.

"I feel sad they did not want to be pets," Aneta said as they neared the bushes.

"We tried though. I guess that's better than hauling them off to be put down. We learned a lot." Esther sounded as though she were trying to make herself feel better.

Sunny and Aneta set down their shelter so it faced the fence but left enough room for the cats to get through the circle. "And we're still helping them. I just wanted them all to be adopted and have a great life."

"You're giving them a better life than they had before," the Cat Woman reminded them.

After placing the shelters, Aneta straightened. "Now we make cute litter boxes." Then her smile ran wide. "And then—"

C. P. shot his fist in the air. "Disgusting organic cat treats!"

Vee noticed Mom's Honda and Bill's truck in the parking lot as they turned to head back into the senior center. She ran to greet them, a puzzled expression crossing her face. Was something wrong?

Frank and Nadine came out the senior center doors. "Hey, April and Bill. Thanks for coming. I know you're both busy."

Panic seized Vee. She looked from Mom and her stepdad to Frank and Nadine. No way could she be in trouble. The girls were working with the old people, and they were on target for the Helpful City Festival. The mayor was happy; Mrs. Sissy was happy. Why were Mom and Bill here?

"Let's all go into the Cat Room," Frank said.

The girls, C. P., and Cat Woman had joined Vee.

"What's going on?" Vee heard Sunny whisper to Aneta.

"I do not know," Aneta whispered back.

"We are definitely *not* in trouble," Esther assured them, nudging Vee's arm as they left the parking lot and went inside. "Are we?"

Vee immediately went to Buzz and lifted him out of his cage. He began a most reassuring buzz against her chest where she clutched him.

"Nope, nobody is in trouble," Frank said. "Even though it would be fun to make you think you were."

"Frank," Nadine said in a warning voice, although she was smiling. "Don't drag this out."

"You're no fun," he grumbled then gestured to Mom, who in turn looked at Bill.

Hello? Freaking out here.

"Here's the deal," Bill said, putting his arm around Vee's mom and smiling his wide smile. "We think Vee's found a treasure in Buzz, and he needs to come home with us forever. Paws 'N' Claws has checked us out, and we're okayed." He pulled a worried face. "That is, Vee, if you want him." The grin he flashed told everyone he was kidding.

"Want him? Oh, Buzz!" Vee choked up and looked down at the big-eyed kitten with the tufty ears. The kitten that was *now hers.*

Sunny grabbed Aneta and danced with her as best they could among the tables and chairs. Esther and Cat Woman clapped. "You get a Cat Kit to take home!" Sunny said.

Mine, he's mine. My treasure, my treasure that came out of trouble. She didn't know how long she stood looking into the ever-changing eyes of Buzz. Time stood still. Her slide into the bushes on a *beetle-y* day she thought would never end. The dive into the Dumpster to save Buzz, then him peeking out at her and her knowing she'd have to save him. Her hip was feeling a lot less sore, thank you very much.

She recalled way too many days where he thought all humans were evil and then that insane day *Everything Animal* turned everything upside down. Buzz's eyes were swooping in and out of slits as he dozed. She glanced at Bill. "Good day for treasure," she said and walked over and placed the drowsy kitten in Bill's big hands.

Mom leaned in close. "He's a cutie."

C. P.'s voice broke up the sweet scene. "So when do we get to make the cat treats?"

"Let me get this straight," Mom said, rubbing her face as the three of them sat around the kitchen island for dinner. "You want me to sign a permission slip to have a lock-in sleepover at the *senior center?*" She took a swallow of ice water. "With old people and *cats?*"

"Seniors, Mom," Vee said. "Not old people. *Really.*"

"That would be worth recording," Bill said, helping himself to another slice of real pizza—as in not potato pizza—that Mom had brought home. She'd announced she was done working killer hours and they might as well get used to having her around more. Bill and Vee had cheered.

Vee explained. "Cat Woman, I mean *Gladys*, says the senior citizens liked working with us. There are cots used for disaster preparedness that we'll use."

"Makes sense." Bill wiped his mouth with a napkin. "Your whole project has been like a disaster preparedness project."

The Lock-In:
1. *Decorate the Cat Room*
2. *Cat Woman's surprise*
3. *Food*
4. *Stay up late—sort of*
5. *Breakfast*

Vee slugged him in the arm. After fortifying herself with a few bites of pizza, she delivered her strongest point for signing the permission slip. "And you guys won't have to wake up early to take me to the senior center."

Bill grabbed the permission slip from his wife. "Sold." He signed with a flourish. "Don't get into trouble."

"With senior citizens?" Vee reached for her ice water. "There's as much a chance of that as us ever seeing Flick the cat again."

Mom and Bill and Vee laughed, Vee the hardest.

That evening, over beetling math homework, Vee looked at the first problem, Buzz buzzing in her lap.

> *Find the next three numbers in the pattern:*
> *1) 320, 160, 80, 40*
> *2) 24, 40, 56, 72*

Pattern? Vee began to smile.

Chapter 26

Cute Litter Pans?

I don't think it's going to happen," C. P. said Thursday, holding up yet another attempt to make cute litter pans. He had daubed white shoe polish in dots over a litter pan he'd spray painted black. "Still looks like a painted litter pan." The girls, C. P., and their senior helpers had been trying to come up with "cute" litter pans for more than two hours.

"I think you're right. A litter pan is just a litter pan. You can't dress it up," Esther concurred. She turned to the helpers and the Squadders. "Agreed?"

Vee raised one of Buzz's paws. "Buzz says yes! It's just a litter pan." Little Buzz had completely trapped Mom and Bill under his little velvety paw from the moment he became part of the family. Mom drank her morning coffee with him in her lap. Bill sang crazy songs to Buzz while the kitten waited for him outside the shower. Since Bill went in so early, he got out early from work and so had delivered Buzz to Vee at the senior center in Buzz's own Squad-decorated cardboard carrier. Maybe the little kitten was getting used to it, even though he blew out of there each time, shook himself, and gave everyone the stink eye before washing himself.

She pulled her notebook out of her back pocket and crossed "cute" off the list, pushing Buzz away. He thought all pens were a Feather Freakie and must be attacked. She surveyed their list.

1. *Community cat shelters*
2. *Cat toys*
3. ~~*Cute*~~ *litter boxes*
4. *Face paint and painters*
5. *Cat Kits*
   a. *Bag of kitty litter*
   b. *Feather Freakie*
   c. *Sock 'Ems*
   d. *How to care for a cat brochure (written by Esther)*
6. *Petting Palace—done*

"May I speak with you privately, Gladys?" Mrs. Sissy entered the room and motioned to the Cat Woman, whom the girls just couldn't seem to remember to call by her real name. The two women left the room. Mrs. Sissy no longer glared at them, but she had yet to smile.

"What's that all about?" Sunny wondered as she packed up the painting supplies. "Can we use any of these for the face painting on Friday and Saturday?"

"Shoe polish and spray paint?" Esther looked shocked.

Sunny shrugged. "Oh, probably not, huh?"

"I hope Cat Woman is not in trouble," Aneta said, stacking the cute and uncute litter pans. They would leave the supplies in the Cat Room so the pickleball club could put the Cat Kits together tomorrow.

Cutting it close. Vee thought of her list. The Helpful City Festival began at noon tomorrow. She would wake up early and take the retest. It would seem weird not to see Math Man anymore. A very good weird.

By Monday she would know if she would get to stay in the Accelerated Learning Center or not.

"We're still short someone to run the Petting Palace," she said, looking at the remaining item. "Aneta is selling the cat treats and toys. C. P. will run around telling everyone about the treats. He's obsessed with them. Esther is helping the senior center with their computer presentations of Oakton's history as a helpful city. Sunny is helping that retired art teacher paint cat faces on kids. I'm going to be in the Cat Room directing people to the adoption counselors. So who's going to run the Petting Palace?"

"I would love to," Mrs. Sissy said as she and Cat Woman reentered the room. Vee joined the girls with an astounded expression. *That* was not expected. Vee would have expected Mrs. Sissy to say she knew they wouldn't be organized enough for opening day.

Petting Palace

But what the Cat Woman said next was even more unexpected.

Chapter 27

The Cat Woman Said What?

Sleeping bags and duffels at their feet, the S.A.V.E. Squad—and C. P.—waited in the parking lot as the final people left both the community center, the library, and the senior center.

"Weird," C. P. said, searching through his pockets and retrieving a piece of gum.

"Very," Sunny said, spinning.

"Special," Aneta said, sinking to sit on her sleeping bag.

"Like we're getting away with something," Esther said, arms folded as she watched the exodus.

Vee agreed with them all. Waiting until everyone was out of the community center and other wings of the building and then getting to go in for the rest of the night was pretty cool. Nobody else got to do that.

A few minutes more and then Cat Woman and a small group of the senior volunteers the girls had come to admire stood in the doorway.

"C'mon in!" Cat Woman called. The men and women next to her beckoned. The kids didn't need to be invited twice. They grabbed their stuff and headed in.

"We'll set up our bivouac here." The enormous man led them to the auditorium.

"Means a sort of campsite," whispered C. P. At the girls' *how-do-you-know-that?* look, he added, "You have to blow one up in the *Army of Wun* game."

Vee looked around. A bunch of cots were scattered around the room. Some people had assembled little camping areas with an extension cord, a table, and a lamp. Some cots had inflatable mattresses. A sound system sat on one side of the large room playing some sort of oldies. Another table was heaped with various decorations: crepe paper, ribbons, tinsel. Material to decorate the Cat Room.

"Hello, girls!" a familiar voice sounded from behind them. Mrs. Sissy was there with the mayor. "Look who I brought. My sister can't resist a party." They were carrying suitcases. The mayor carried an inflatable mattress in a bag.

"Food first!" called a lady, and everyone, C. P. leading the way, surged over to the three tables filled with slow cookers. The side door to the auditorium was open, and smells from the barbecue filtered in.

"This is such a neat idea. Maybe we should do it as a senior event," remarked one woman, passing with a plate piled high.

"Wait and see if you can walk tomorrow, then decide," advised her friend.

Afterward the seniors and the girls set to decorating the Cat Room. Hermann stood on the ladder, and the girls handed up streamers. Next came the banner: THE GREAT CAT CAPER ADOPTION EVENT. That was hung outside the senior center, above the doors. The air was full of autumn. Vee sniffed deeply. What could be the surprise that Cat Woman kept hinting at? She'd been grinning at the girls since they'd entered the senior center. Inside the Cat Room, Aneta neatly lettered name cards for each of the Paws 'N' Claws cats and Momma Cat, decorating around the names with cat faces and dots. She also taped a typed paragraph about the personality of the cat.

"Sunny," she said, taking another card to work on. "What do you think Gladys is thinking up for us?"

Sunny shrugged as she arranged the piles of Cat Kits in a pyramid over in the adoption corner. She stepped back to look. "Yay for catness," she said. In an aside to Vee, "What do *you* think the surprise is?"

"Good work, girl," Hermann said as he passed with an armful of pillows sewn by the seniors. The enormous man carried an equally large armful.

After she had arranged the chairs and pillows in the Petting Palace, Esther looked over Aneta's shoulder. "Great, 'Neta! That will show people what their personalities are like."

"We want them to find their treasure in a forever home," Aneta said, carefully lettering the name "Tux" for a black-and-white cat that looked like it was wearing a tuxedo.

Frank and Nadine brought in cat carriers with the twenty cats up for adoption with Momma Cat. Since Buzz was adopted, Momma Cat had gone to live at Frank and Nadine's until the adoption event. The traps had been removed from the Cat Room.

In no time at all, the adoption center was complete. The seniors and the girls took a last look at the cats in their colorfully decorated cages with the name cards, the streamers gently moving in the air currents as they hung from wires strung from one end of the room to the other. The Petting Palace beckoned in one corner, the adoption center right nearby. Yes, thought Vee as they closed the door, the Great Cat Caper would be a stellar event. *Tomorrow will be a great day for treasure.*

She stopped abruptly; Sunny collided into her. Vee sniffed. Did she smell mouthwash?

"What?" Sunny asked, backing up.

"Do you smell mouthwash?"

"Oh, c'mon, Vee. Tomorrow's the festival. We've done it! This is supposed to be fun!" Sunny pulled her along.

Maybe she was borrowing trouble as one of the pickleball ladies liked to say. She brushed away worries of mouthwash.

Chapter 28

Squadders on a Roll

Gladys is looking for you girls," said the enormous man as they headed back toward the auditorium where they could hear music. "She's in the arts and crafts room."

Cat Woman was rummaging in a closet when the girls arrived. They'd left C. P. prowling the food table and dancing to the music with the seniors. He was a strange boy, that one.

As the older woman turned and greeted them, she pulled out two large plastic tubs. "Thought you girls would like something to do other than dance with old people. Have at it!" She gestured to the tubs.

Sunny ran to the first tub and pulled off the lid. Esther grabbed the second and did the same. They plunged in and began pulling out— roller skates and helmets? But these were not the in-line skates Vee had used before. These were four wheels, two in front and two in back in a leather boot that laced up high. The skates were red with white and blue stars. The helmets looked almost like turtle shells flipped over. The helmet colors matched the skates, each one with a different name on the front: Sissy, Napoleon, Princess, and Queenie, along with others.

"Whoa, yayness." Sunny was pulling off her sneakers and trying on skates. "Where did you get these?" The other girls hung back, looking to Cat Woman for answers. Maybe the Cat Woman really was crazy.

"Thirty years ago Oakton had a roller derby team. I was the captain. Good memories."

"These are so cool!" Sunny raved. "Why didn't you tell us about these before?"

"We were pretty proud of our team. Didn't want you to make fun of it."

Would they have? Vee hoped not.

"Who's 'we'?" Esther was now trying on skates.

Cat Woman said, "The mayor, Mrs. Sissy, and my daughter. She was barely twenty-one. It was the last time we did something together."

Something's not right with her daughter. Vee did the quick math and then laughed at herself. Me doing quick math. Thirty years plus twenty-one. Cat Woman's daughter would be about fifty or so years old. Her daughter must have died for Cat Woman to demonstrate that kind of sadness.

"And getting sad is not why I opened the closet. Get going, girls."

"Um," Aneta said.

What are we going to do with roller skates?

"It's dark out now, Gladys," Esther said as though talking to a little kid.

Cat Woman's smile grew wider. "I know." Standing in the doorway, she turned and said over her shoulder, "You got permission to skate anywhere you want in the entire community center." Then she was gone.

For a moment, the only sounds were of the party in the auditorium. Then Aneta, Esther, and Vee leaped on the skates and began pulling them on, pulling them off, and handing them around until they were all on skates. Sunny, already on hers, helped. All the while they chattered about how nobody would ever believe they were doing this.

"How cool is this?" Sunny took a tentative push off on her right foot and slid smoothly over the bare floor. "Yeow! We're the only kids on the *planet* that have permission to skate inside!" Another push off, and she was circling the room faster and faster, pumping her arms up and down like she was flying. "Wee-hah!"

Aneta was the next behind. Esther and Vee scrambled to stand, unsteadily at first, then clutching hands and shrieking, they gained more confidence until they circled themselves and grinned.

"Out?" Vee said. She stood closest to the door.

"Out!" the Squad chorused.

They were in the hall and flying fast. They shot down one wing and then another. They soon learned the fastest way to stop was to run into something, preferably not each other. That happened, too. A game of tag morphed out of chasing and shrieks. Piercing screams echoed in the library and the community center halls. Then they tried four across, linking arms and speeding down one wing and crouching and leaning to make the turn into the next wing.

Crash!

"Okay, that needs a little work," Esther said from the bottom of the pile.

More than an hour later, they had perfected that turn and had graduated to spinning and throwing each other. One girl would skate. A second would skate at her. The first girl would grab the outstretched arm, sit back, and pull. The second girl would screech and be swung in a tight circle, flung back the way she'd come. That moved to two girls in the hall and two swings and flip arounds. More screaming.

When they finally stopped to slowly roll to the auditorium for drinks for dry throats, Aneta summed it up best, Vee thought. "I will never forget the Great Cat Caper."

"This is the coolest," Sunny agreed.

"Talk about reward for a good job," Esther added. "I would never in a kazillion years think Mrs. Sissy would let us do this."

Vee grinned. "Are you sure she did?"

But when they entered the auditorium, Mrs. Sissy came over, wide smile in place. "Well? Did you girls enjoy our little surprise?"

The music stopped, and the seniors gathered round them.

"Did we ever!" Sunny burst out.

"I liked it," Aneta supplied, her face still pink from the spinning and shrieking.

"Thank you," Esther said to the group, who all smiled back.

"It was the best. Nothing could be more exciting," Vee said. Even the day the *Everything Animal* producer and the cats went berserk wasn't as crazy as this. Tomorrow would probably be a little boring, even though she was determined to help the cats find forever homes.

The seniors had one more surprise for them. After the dance floor cleared, Hermann, Gunny, and the pickleball club people set up obstacle courses for the girls to run in the auditorium. They skated around tables and chairs, dodging the soccer balls their friends rolled in their path. This round of skating left them with floor burns, skinned knees, and even more hysterics. The laughing and shouting bounced off the room walls and made it sound as though there were a thousand roller skaters and obstacle makers.

Vee had no idea of the time when the S.A.V.E. Squad collapsed at one end of the room, breathless.

"I can't move," panted Aneta, lying flat on her back, chest heaving.

"My feet are gonna fall off." Sunny pulled off her skates and rubbed her feet. "How many miles did we skate?"

"A kazillion," Esther replied, sliding down the wall until only her head and shoulders propped up against it.

Vee was too breathless to add anything. She finally felt like the trouble that had dogged her since school began had been spun out of her. Her arms ached from grabbing and being grabbed, and it felt great.

The seniors left by twos and threes until it was Hermann, Mrs. Sissy, the mayor, and the Cat Woman saying good night and heading to their cots and inflatable mattresses.

"Nobody parties like senior citizens," Sunny said, her words slurring slightly as she staggered sock-footed to her cot and dropped into it. She didn't say another word.

"And tomorrow is the next adventure," Vee said with a yawn that almost dislocated her jaw.

Sleep drifted in like wisps of fog as soon as her head touched the flat pillow covered by a paper pillowcase.

Thank You for taking my mind off the retest. "Bless Buzz, especially Flick and all his buddies. . ." was the last thing she remembered praying.

Chapter 29

No So Purr-fect

"Veelie, I want to take you to breakfast for brain food before your test, not spend the time looking at cats." Dad stood by the tail end of the SUV. Vee stood on the senior center steps. She'd been up early enough to see everyone else still sprawled in sleep around the auditorium. Mrs. Sissy had told her she'd set her watch for the others to wake, so Vee wouldn't have to.

"I just want you to see what I've been doing. Are you coming later then?"

He hesitated. Vee knew that meant he had no intention of coming to the Helpful City Festival. She wanted to feel mad so she wouldn't cry, but decided instead to look at the treasure of Dad here now.

"Since you won't be back later, please come in now."

Another long moment. Dad looked at his watch then flicked the remote at the SUV. "We'll have to do a drive-thru for your breakfast. And we have to hurry, Vee."

"Right, Dad." She turned with him as he came up the steps.

"We have twenty cats that are ready for adopting. We've done the cutest Cat Kits for everyone who adopts a cat. Then people can buy other things for their cats or people they know who have cats." She made sure to mention that the *Everything Animal* show, a *national* TV show, would be rolling their cameras at the start of the Great Cat Caper Adoption Event.

He grunted and looked at his watch. "We have to be sure to get you a water bottle for the test. It helps your brain to have plenty of water. You've worked hard for this, Vee. I'm sure you'll do well."

Oh. Dad was in a different "room." He probably wouldn't even see the cats when he was standing in front of them. She took a deep breath. Was there the tiniest whiff of mouthwash? She did a quick scan. Nobody in the hall. "Sure, then I won't ever have to see Math Man again."

"Vee."

"Sorry, Dad. Here's the Cat Room. Prepare for some awesome catness." She flung open the door with a grand gesture of her arm. "Ta-dah!"

The Cat Room was still decorated, but there was not a cat in sight. The carriers stood empty, doors swinging wide.

Chapter 30

Catnapped!

I can't think," Esther said, clutching her head.

"Too many people giving dumb advice," Sunny complained, looking again in the Cat Room like she might find all the cats magically there again.

"We must find them." Aneta had been saying that since Vee ran to awaken the girls after finding the cats missing.

Vee's brain was whirling. She couldn't get the smell of mouthwash out of her mind. Right before she opened the door, she'd smelled that mouthwash and thought it odd that weird lady's smell would still be around so long after the senior center closed. If only Vee had done something then. But what?

"Vee, time to go. You'll be late for the retest." Dad was standing by the senior center door, stepping aside every time someone else ran in or out yelling, "The cats are gone!"

"Dad, I can't go. I have to help find the cats," Vee said, swallowing hard. What if it had been Buzz still in one of those carriers?

"Vee."

"Dad, please. It's important."

"School is more important than cats. Let's go." He stepped toward the door. "If you're not in the SUV in five minutes, I'm leaving. And you're headed back to regular sixth grade. Is that what you want?"

"Dad—" What could she say? "My want-to has been ramped up for weeks. It's just, well—"

Dad's face looked like he couldn't decide whether to yell or cry. It scared Vee.

"I guess—" he paused. "Heather's been telling me—" He shook his head. "I give up."

The lump in her throat made it impossible to reply. Dad left.

The girls encircled her with hugs.

"Okay, what do we do now?" She had to get a list going in her head or she would explode. For so many weeks, the retest had been the most important thing. Not anymore. Tomorrow she would have to think about life in the regular sixth grade. But not today.

1. *Look by the Dumpster.*
2. *Look by the lake.*
3. *Look for loose cats.*
4. *Look for someone carrying cats?*

"Time to head outside," Esther said.

Vee and Aneta nodded.

"Skates." Sunny dashed off toward the auditorium. She returned, skates and helmets hanging over both arms. "We can cover more ground faster on skates."

Wordless, they yanked on skates and helmets. After checking to make sure each other's skates and helmets were securely fastened, they skated to the entrance of the senior center.

"Last night was perfect. The Cat Room looked perfect. The seniors' surprise was perfect. It was a perfect night," Sunny said, her voice trembling.

"Right. Now it's not perfect." Esther sounded fierce, her hands on her hips. Sunny reached for the crash bar so they could plunge through the doorway, cling to the rail to get down the steps, and start their search in the great outdoors. Instead, as she leaned on the bar, it opened suddenly and she fell forward. Right into Ginger, the producer for *Everything Animal*. The two fell over, and the camera crew tossed their cameras to their shoulders and began filming.

"Not *now*, guys," Ginger cried, struggling to push Sunny off her.

In the disaster, Vee had completely forgotten about *Everything Animal*.

"Dumpster first." Vee pulled Sunny to her feet, greeted Ginger with, "Hello, welcome to the Great Cat Caper," and rolled down the handicap ramp. *How do you have a Great Cat Caper with no cats?*

"I want all this on video!" Ginger directed her crew to follow the girls.

What? Not only were they failing their project, but it was going to be recorded for national TV? *Beetle.* That was simply it. *Beetle, beetle, beetle.* The girls rolled their eyes at each other then shrugged. No time to waste.

A young couple in running clothes had paused to catch their breath.

"Have you seen anyone carrying a lot of cats?" Aneta asked.

The couple looked puzzled. "Nope, just a lady with a baby stroller," the man said, and the two ran off.

In a straight line across, the Squad rolled toward the bushes Vee remembered so well. She thought of Buzz, safe and probably still asleep at her house. She felt guilty being glad he had been adopted early and wasn't in the Cat Room when the unthinkable happened. The missing cats were pets, not Dumpster cats. They would be afraid to be out in what to them was the wild. Who could—*how* could—they have gotten out?

No cats in the bushes or around the Dumpster. Not even the cat condo dwellers. The crew swarmed around their disappointed faces.

"The lake," Sunny said, turning away from one camera only to find another in her face. "Fast," she added with a bit of a grin. Without a word to one another, they turned and took off out of the parking lot, leaving the camera crew behind. Squatting down on their heels and wrapping their arms around their knees, they rode the paved road to the gravel where they tipped over. After brushing each other off, they carefully stepped down the gravel road, holding on to each other. Calling the cat names they remembered, they peeked under bushes and even looked under the dock where it sat on the sand. No cats.

"The park." Aneta turned and led the way back up the road.

When they hit the paved, steep road again, Sunny dropped to the ground, pulling off her skates. "Skate's off. Hill's too steep to get going on skates." The other three obeyed. Then they ran up the road, where the crew stood filming their approach.

"Wave and look happy," Esther ordered. The girls pasted big smiles on their faces and sat down to put on their skates and helmets.

"Aneta and I will go one way," Vee said, lacing her skates quickly and jamming the helmet on her head, fastening it snugly under her chin.

"We'll meet you from the other side," Sunny said. Esther bobbed her head in agreement.

Vee and Aneta held hands as they skated along the parkway. The crew had wised up and had sprinted for their truck, driving along Park Street with one camera operator leaning out the window. Vee looked to the left and Aneta toward the wide expanse of the park. She was getting close to crying. Dad was mad at her. Heather would smile and tell her she loved her heart. Mom would say she'd gone overboard on cats and had lost perspective. Bill? What would Bill say? *Great day for treasure.* They were looking for treasure, all right. But would they find it?

"When you look for treasure," Vee muttered, her eyes scanning back and forth, "you have to follow a map, some sort of guide." Beside her, she could hear Aneta softly whispering and knew she was praying. A spring of comfort washed up her spine. What would she do without the S.A.V.E. Squad as friends?

"You are my Treasure," Vee prayed, too. "Be our Guide. Um, please?"

The two girls met up with Sunny and Esther who also had nothing to report. They crossed the street to The Sweet Stuff and asked if anyone had seen cats running around. No one had, but everyone expressed concern about the upcoming adoption event.

"Now what?" Esther asked when they were back on the opposite side of the street and looking at the community center that revealed no cats.

Having cameras standing around a person was kinda distracting. Vee wished she'd never contacted *Everything Animal.* Who took the cats? Mouthwash lady? Why? And what would she do with them if she did take them? Who *was* she?

The park was rapidly filling with booths and a sound stage. Kids from every school in the city roamed the park, some carrying signs, laptops, and materials for their final service-learning presentation. Vee felt tears prick the back of her eyes, and as she dashed them away, she noticed Aneta was quietly crying and Esther's face was red, blotchy like Frank's, but Esther was holding back tears. Sunny had the red-rimmed rabbit eyes. Nobody had a plan. They were in big trouble.

The lead camera operator lowered her camera and said, " 'Kay, guys, let's cut it. Nothing here."

The lady was right.

Chapter 31

Flick Shows Up

Vee spotted a familiar tail coming across the park. "That's not Flick, is it?" she asked the girls, narrowing her eyes to get a better look in the morning sun. Flick never came out in the open like that.

"Sure looks like him, the way he scoots along with his black tail up straight like he's leading a parade," Sunny said, also shading her eyes.

The cat stopped a safe distance from the group on the path. Out of the corner of her eye, Vee noticed the camera people slip the cameras back up on their shoulders. The cat's tail quirked near the top so it turned the whole tail into a question mark. That was the question for sure, Vee thought. *Where are the cats?*

Flick turned half away and then turned his head. The tail questioned. *Good day for treasure* came suddenly to Vee. She and the cat locked gazes. *You can't be doing what I think you're doing.*

Flick went the tail.

The cat moved a few glide-y steps onto the sidewalk and looked back again. *Sometimes you don't have to know what you don't know to know it.* It made no sense and all kinds of sense. Vee's skates were moving. "I might be crazy," she said to the girls as she slowly approached the suddenly still flick-tailed cat. "But I think Flick is trying to tell us something."

"Crazy is all we've got," Sunny said. The other two agreed. The girls joined Vee, and in a flash, Flick had flipped around and was down the sidewalk, weaving in and out of people.

"C'mon!" Esther said to the camera crew. "Keep up!"

The cat kept up an easy trot. The difficult part for the girls was keeping Flick in sight with all the commotion of setting up for the festival. Trucks were backing across the sidewalk. People were carrying cartons and wheeling hand trucks of boxes.

"Where did he go?"

"Oh, look, I see his tail!"

"For pizza sake, Flick, quit ducking behind stuff!"

At the edge of the park, Flick seemed determined to keep going. But where? There was nothing except the side of the community center, and it was clear of cats.

"Guys, I think he's leading us on a merry cat chase." Sunny's voice was discouraged. She stopped by the Van Go Meals booth and the free blood pressure check table. Three girls younger than the Squad were setting out piles of handouts and setting a can of vegetables on each pile to keep them from blowing away.

A little girl who, Vee thought, was probably supposed to be attached to one of the older girls, had wandered away and spied Flick. Although Vee wasn't a good judge of kids' ages, she looked a lot younger than the Twin Terrors.

"Uh-oh," she said. Once Flick saw her, the flighty flick-tailed feline would vanish up a tree or around the building and they'd be back to no plan. And lots of trouble.

"Stay away from the kitty," Esther said to the little girl, sounding very friendly. She walked toward the girl with her hands out. Flick saw the little girl. His tail stiffened, and he puffed up.

Vee held her breath. Would he bolt?

"Yes, little girl," Aneta chimed in, stepping to Esther's side to further block her view of the feline.

The little girl stopped, stuck her index finger in her mouth, and stared. Aneta and Esther took a step toward her. The finger came out of the mouth. "Stranger danger! Stranger danger!" the little girl shrieked, pointing the finger toward the two girls. "Stranger danger. Stranger danger!"

Then everyone on the planet was looking at them. The girls at the table glared, the sister grabbed her little sister. The adults at the table pulled out cell phones. Passersby halted and began to form a menacing circle around the S.A.V.E. Squad. *Big trouble,* Vee thought, still keeping an eye on Flick. The Dumpster cat had amazingly not moved. He didn't look scared anymore. He'd curled his tail around his body and appeared to be enjoying the show.

Stalemate. It was a language-arts vocabulary word that fit right now. Can't go forward, can't go back. If they followed Flick, people would probably chase them and call the police. If they stayed, Flick would take off and they'd never know if he *was* leading them to the catnapped cats.

"Vhat you kids doing?" It was Hermann. Vee had never been so glad to see the gruff old man.

"The cats are stolen!"

"Flick is leading us to them!"

"These people think we're creepy!"

Hermann stood unfazed by the words hurled at him. He spoke to the adults manning the tables and assured them, indeed, the girls were crazy but harmless and dispersed the crowd. Then he looked at Flick. Flick looked at Hermann. "Vell, den, show de kids de kots!" he said.

Flick stood, stretched each vertebra from the tail to his neck in a slow, sinuous arc, and took off running, tail straight up.

"Go! Go! Go!" Sunny was the first to follow with Vee, Aneta, and Esther stringing out behind.

Flick led them across the street and down the side of the community center. At the end of the community center stood a fence that surrounded the emergency generators and other mechanical equipment. Vee could see it through the slats. While it was taller than the girls, Flick dug in his claws and was up and over the top. The girls lined up and peered through the slats.

"I see machinery."

"I see Flick."

"I see a stroller. Weird. Flick climbed in, and the whole thing is shaking."

"There's a stroller in there?" Vee flashed back to when they first burst out of the senior center. Vee had asked a couple in running clothes if they had seen cats. *"Nope,"* she remembered their reply. *"Just a woman pushing a baby stroller."*

Mouthwash lady.

"How are we going to get over the fence?" Aneta stretched up and dug her sneakered toes into the slats. She slipped back and rubbed her hands together. "Ouch." Sounds of meowing came from the stroller. Aneta peeked in. "They're beginning to crawl out of the stroller!" She looked at the camera crew, who kept their eyeballs locked to their cameras. "Help?"

"Sorry," one said. "We're observers, not participators."

Esther gave them the stink eye and said, "I'll go get Frank. He's got to have keys!" She ran off.

Aneta's eye was glued to a space between the slats and chain link. "If they all get out, they'll start climbing the fence and we'll never get them back for the Great Cat Caper."

Vee thought fast. "We can't wait till Esther gets back with Frank. We don't even know if Frank is at the senior center yet." They hadn't come this far to have their project disappear over the wall. Those cats needed to be someone's treasure.

"Shoulders!" Sunny pointed to Aneta. "You're the tallest. Except we're all too tall. What we need is someone—"

"—who's a shrimp." C. P.'s scratchy voice jumped in. He had appeared, finishing off a maple bar. Wiping his hands on his cargo shorts, he inquired, "What is it with you girls and fences?"

Sunny squatted and cupped her hands. "Put your foot in there, and I'll shoot you up to Aneta's shoulders."

C. P. stepped forward, placed his left foot in Sunny's cupped hands and his hands on her shoulders. "Ready."

Sunny sniffed. "C. P., did you just put sticky maple bar stuff on my shirt?" Grunting, Sunny staggered to her feet, and C. P. flew up toward Aneta. He landed on his knees, thudding on her shoulders.

"C. P.!" Aneta wailed. "Hurry! You are short but you are *heavy*."

He struggled to get his balance. "Quit moving! Hey!" He looked down at Vee. "Get your hand off my shorts!"

The camera crew would love that sound bite. "Don't be creepy. I'm trying to keep you from falling," Vee said.

C. P. got up on one foot and then the other. Aneta groaned and wobbled. The boy placed his hands on the fence. He took a deep breath, leaned forward, and did a slow roll over the fence—head first, his short, bare legs tucked in tightly to his body.

"CEEEEEPEEEEEE!" shrieked Vee and Sunny. They ran to the fence and peered through. "Are you dead?"

Chapter 32

Surprise Help

Sunny rounded on the camera crew. "If he's dead, so are you, busters!"

"Lemme check," came a shaky voice from the other side. There was a muffled *ouch* and the crunch of gravel. "No. I just let go of the top bar too late. I think I'm taller now. Cool."

"The cats?" Vee asked.

"How many should there be?"

"Twenty."

Sounds of breathy counting. "Twenty-one."

"That's because Flick is in there," Vee said.

"Make that twenty. One cat high-tailed it over the fence."

"Flick," Vee said.

"Uhh, hurry up and get us out of here," C. P. said. "They're all looking at me and then the fence. I think they're going to use me as a ladder. Hurry *up!*"

Oops. Vee, Aneta, and Sunny swapped looks. How were they going to get C. P. and the cats out? Sunny covered her mouth to smother a laugh. Vee clutched her head, and Aneta's eyes got big. The camera crew chuckled.

"Girls!" Frank yelled, with Esther following behind, gasping and leaning to put her hands on her knees to catch her breath. He unlocked the gate. "There are people right behind with cat carriers. Just keep those dratted cats from sneaking out the gate when I open it." He and the girls slipped inside and began rubbing bellies, coaxing cats off the slatted fence, and telling C. P. how wonderful he was. He assured them he knew.

Heather, Dad, and the Twin Terrors appeared in the doorway of the fence.

"Dad!" Vee was startled. She held a cat in each hand.

"Vee the B!" The Twin Terrors each opened their carrier, and she popped in the cats. The boys closed the carriers and quickly brought two more in. Those little guys could move fast. Not a single cat escaped on their watch.

Dad and Heather rounded up the rest of the cats, placing them in the carriers. Some of the cats weren't too happy with sharing a carrier, but the hissing and spitting was soon over.

Heather and the boys left with Frank and the rest of the Squad. The crew followed, still filming. Dad and Vee closed and locked the gate and walked back to the community center.

"What are you doing here, Dad?"

"Trying not to be a jerk," Dad said. "You remember I told you I wanted to talk to you about your want-to?"

"Yeah."

"Well, Heather has been showing me that revving up your want-to isn't always the wisest way to go. Like me spending too much time at work, trying to be a big shot so my family can have cool things. Like I did with you. I don't want to do that anymore."

"That's good for the Twin Terrors," Vee said slowly.

"I hope it will be good for you as well. I'm sorry I made a big deal about the retest. I'm sorry I didn't show up for your cat project. I'm sorry I treated your project like it wasn't worth anything." He stopped and put a hand on each shoulder.

Here we go with the hand on the shoulder again. It must be an adult thing.

"I won't say I won't ever let you down again, but today's not the day. Will you accept that?"

Vee flung her arm around her dad's waist. "Oh, Dad."

Chapter 33

Where's Bill?

The Squad stood in the Cat Room, admiring the newly returned adoptables in their decorated cages. Vee watched her family—Heather, Dad, and the boys who were strutting around telling about their role in the rescue. The stories got bigger with each telling.

The seniors fussed over C. P. with free food from all the booths and a bottle of water. As he sat in one of the chairs in the adoption center, swinging his feet and polishing off an orange, he suddenly spoke. "Hey!"

The girls turned around from straightening the scattered tables from the mouthwash lady's flight with all the cats.

"How were you going to get me and the cats *back* over that fence?" he asked, accusing.

Sunny looked at Aneta. Aneta looked at Esther. Esther looked at Vee.

He shook his head and stuffed the rest of the orange in his mouth. "Girlthhs!" he said thickly.

The rest of Friday and all of Saturday turned out to be a good day for treasure. The Petting Palace was busy with a smiling, laughing

Mrs. Sissy, who quickly memorized every bio on every cat and shared it with all the petters. Twice the adoption center had lines. The Cat Kits sold out quickly. The organic cat treats were a hit. Ginger was clearly thrilled with the footage of the dramatic rescue.

It was the Feather Freakies and Sock 'Ems that the *Everything Animal* producer loved the most, however. "They are just so cool," she said, holding Momma Cat on her lap and dangling the Freakie in front of her. Momma Cat responded quickly, slapping out a paw and capturing the feather and then batting it back and forth between her paws. Soon she had rolled onto her back in Ginger's lap and had all four paws involved. "I love this cat. Too bad I live in New York."

Vee watched Mrs. Sissy watching Ginger with Momma Cat. "I think Momma Cat already has a fan here."

"Yeah, it would be tough to fly her back. She wouldn't like it. I'm going to go to a no-kill cat rescue in the city. Can I show them the Freakie and the Sock 'Em? They could use them for an activity in their humane education."

"Of course," Esther said, looking pleased.

Before she left, the producer asked if she could e-mail the Squad with pictures once she adopted a cat. The girls agreed it would be very cool to see a New York City cat that was now an *Everything Animal* treasure.

Ginger finished up her interviews and final footage, then the crew packed up. She seemed to linger after they left. Finally, she blushed a bit. "You girls have such a great life here and do wonderful things. Being a kid is so trouble-free, it makes me want to be a kid again."

The Squad just smiled. Vee forced herself *not* to roll her eyes.

Where *was* he? All around her, the festival was closing down. People were taking down long tables, backing cars and trailers into the park and loading, and yelling good-byes. Vee felt forgotten. The senior center had closed early with every cat adopted. Tonight there would be a big concert in the park, but the Squad was meeting at her house to celebrate a successful Great Cat Caper. Bill had said he'd be there by now to pick her up.

The lightness that had settled on Vee since the cats had been found began to fade. What was it about dads and semi-dads and being on time? She had pretty much figured by now that Bill was a Super Bill. *Guess not.* She wished she hadn't left her ATP at home.

The blast of an air horn jolted her, and she ran around the corner of the senior center to see what it was. A gigantic diesel truck without a trailer was rolling toward her down the road from the main street. Bill was leaning out the window yelling, "Vee girl! Hey, are you still here?"

"I'm here! I'm here! You're here! You're late!" she waved, all heaviness banished. He *came.*

As soon as the rig slowed to a stop, Bill swung down. His face was scraped and bloody, and he moved as though he'd had a run-in with an entire football team. He bent down and scooped her up into a bear hug. For once Vee didn't mind. Even if she wasn't a huggy person. When he set her down, she slugged his arm and felt better. He winced.

"What happened to your face? Did you get into a fight with a barbed-wire fence?"

He motioned for her to get in, and she smiled. Going home in style. She climbed up and hitched across the front to the passenger side. Bill slowly got in, swung the door shut, and they rolled around onto Park Street to make a circle around the park and head home.

"I was working on a rig, and something went wonky with the lift. It just dropped."

"Dropped on you!" Vee drew in a sharp breath. "Why aren't you dead?"

"Not my time," he said, although the smile was shaky. "The lift just stopped as soon as it touched my face. It should have crushed me. It took the guys a while to stabilize everything so I could get pulled out without everything collapsing."

Remembering all her dark thoughts about dads and being left, Vee swallowed a lump in her throat. This time she patted Bill's arm instead of punching it. She and Mom had almost lost Super Bill. That would be worse than *beetle-y*.

At the STOP sign on Park, Bill looked for traffic both ways and then down at Vee. "I'm sorry I was late. I won't promise I won't ever let you down, Vee girl, 'cause I know I probably will—"

"But today is not the day," she finished for him. And smiled.

Chapter 34

Treasure Found

Later, in Bill's tiny backyard full of people, the barbecue, and Buzz's new cat playhouse that Bill had just finished that day, Sunny looked concerned. "So what happens to the Accelerated Learning Center?"

"That's the coolest cat cage," Jacob said, standing near the playhouse where Buzz roamed up and down the ramps and batted various hanging Freakies and Sock 'Ems. Vee now knew he was Jacob because out of all the tiny freckles he had on his pale face, he had one by his left ear that was slightly larger. Joshua didn't.

"Remember, don't tease the cat," Dad said. He and Heather sat side by side in the chairs they'd brought. Vee had reminded everyone to bring their own chairs.

"Maybe we should keep Buzz out here with us and put the boys in the playhouse," Heather remarked, and everyone laughed. The Terrors thought it was a great idea and had to be instructed not to open the playhouse and climb in.

"I get to stay in the ALC!" Vee said happily.

C. P. was patrolling the table filled with chips, sour cream onion dip, and yes, baked potatoes with bowls of weird toppings. "Vee gets special treatment. Not that the ALC is so great."

"No, I don't!" she flashed until she saw his sneaky grin. "Oh, close your yap, C. P."

"Spill," Esther said, sitting next to Aneta and The Fam. The rest of her family was sprinkled around the yard in various types of chairs.

"I'm—," Joshua began.

"—hungry," Jacob finished.

"Just about done," Bill promised.

"The guidance counselor said I was a type of student they would like to see more often." Vee turned her head toward the twins who were softly chanting, "Vee the B, Vee the B" as they walked in circles around each other. "Guys." They collapsed on the grass and pretended to be asleep. *If only.*

Mom picked up the story. She was assisting Bill at the grill where hot dogs and hamburgers were coming off and headed toward buns on the table. "Long story short, she can retest Monday after school. The guidance counselor said"—she looked fondly at Vee—"Vee showed her priorities in life skills with choosing to help her friends and the cause to which she was committed."

"Yayness!" Sunny clapped.

"What will happen to Vee if she does not pass?" Aneta passed a red plastic cup of punch to her grand.

"If she passes, she's in the Accelerated Learning Center. If she doesn't, she will still stay in the Accelerated Learning Center and go to the regular math class. If that's the case, she'll be a test case to see how it works. The district is thinking to expand the acceptance criteria into the accelerated center so those kids get the options to move ahead while shoring up their weak subject."

"You girls did a great job on the Great Cat Caper," Dad jumped in after Mom finished. "Heather and I talked it over, and while we don't think a cat is in our future—boys!" The twins settled down. "We decided that whenever our family eats at Burger Mania, where we do a lot, we're going to stop by the grocery store and pick up a cat meal to donate to Paws 'N' Claws." He turned to Vee. "But I would like to know what happened to the woman who snatched the cats and dumped them over the fence. Did they catch her?"

The girls were silent so long, C. P. spoke up.

"It's a bummer story," he said. "The mouthwash lady—"

"Mouthwash lady?" Mr. and Mrs. Martin said together.

"Vee kept smelling a certain mouthwash whenever it seemed something was just a little off at the Cat Room," Bill explained. Vee had dumped the whole story on him on the way home in the diesel cab. "Turns out it was a woman who was kind of skulking around the senior center."

"Who turned out to be Cat Woman's daughter," Vee added.

"Cat Woman—I mean, Gladys—was very involved in helping cats when her daughter was about twenty-one. Gladys said her daughter started mistreating the cats, and Gladys had to move her out of the house. She hadn't seen her daughter for years."

"Nobody recognized her?" Aneta's mom spoke up. Vee figured she was thinking like the attorney she was. Somebody was probably going to get sued for letting a crazy person run around the senior center.

"She wouldn't have hurt us," Vee hastened to say, and Aneta's mom's face relaxed. "It was the cats. They found her at the Paws 'N' Claws office, vandalizing it. After they arrested her, she said she'd planned to pull the cats back up from the fence with the rope attached to the stroller and dump them somewhere her mother would never find them."

"They would have died," Aneta said, her face shocked.

Vee nodded. "People think cats can go back to the wild. Not true. They need us."

Mr. Martin held up his hands. "Okay, don't you girls get started again. Sunny's been lecturing us for weeks on cats and people not spaying and neutering. Our family is continuing our service-learning project for the rest of the year."

"I'm going to be a photographer of the animals at Paws 'N' Claws! I'll take photos of the new cats coming for the website, the lost ones found, and do different photo spreads. My family is going to keep the cat toys stocked and host a pet food drive with our youth group when the weather gets cold."

Bill set the platter on the table. "Ready!"

Everyone settled around the picnic table, several card tables, a church banquet table, and a white, round plastic table. But they all fit. They joined hands at Heather's request. Vee asked her stepmother to pray.

"Thank You, Lord, for the food we are about to eat. Help us find our place in You in every moment."

Startled, Vee squeezed her eyes shut. *Place.* She'd found more than a spot. In God—as His treasure. In her family—both of them. In her school. And she knew now that she'd already had a spot in the S.A.V.E. Squad from the first time they'd disagreed. She opened one eye and found the Squad peeking at her. They shared a Squad smile.

Soon everyone had stuffed themselves and was lying around— except the Twin Terrors and Sunny who were playing with the cat. Sunny was keeping a very close eye on how they handled Buzz, Vee was glad to see. Sunny knew little brothers.

Vee sat in a patch of sunlight that had seemed to shine just for her. What a weekend. What a start to school. She couldn't wait to get to school on Monday. When the guidance counselor had talked to her and Mom, she had asked Vee if she could handle walking out of the learning center every day for math if she didn't pass the placement test.

After thinking about it, Vee had replied that if the counselor had asked her the first day of school, she would have said, "No way." Now? She'd given it her best shot. If she needed help, she needed help.

From her sunlit spot, she observed Esther and Aneta walk over to Sunny and whisper in her ear. She lifted her head. Sunny picked up Buzz, much to the cries of the Twin Terrors, and walked with the other two girls to Vee.

"We have a surprise for you," Esther said, pulling a small paper bag out of her shorts pocket. "Come on over to the table."

What were they up to? The girls sat at the table. The families looked on from their chairs. The twins pushed in next to Vee, pungent in their sweaty boyness.

Esther nodded at Sunny, who handed Buzz to Vee, cleared her throat, and said dramatically, "We want you to have a memento of the Great Cat Caper. Remember how when school started you kept talking about how you didn't have a spot?"

Vee blushed and avoided looking at her family by holding Buzz like a baby and stroking his tummy. He buzzed contentedly.

"You have a *spot* in the S.A.V.E. Squad," Sunny finished, with an emphasis on *spot*.

Esther tipped the bag open onto the table. A single white bead, oblong, with a large black spot rolled onto the table. "To add to your Squad bracelet."

Picking up the bead, Vee laughed and then hugged her friends. "I have lots of spots now and a place with God. It all started with you guys. This is perfect! Thanks!" She untied the leather cord and slid the bead on, knotting before and after it. She held it up. The girls held theirs up. "To the S.A.V.E. Squad!"

Bill tapped his tongs on the grill and then raised them. "I, too, have a presentation."

Enquiring eyes turned from the girls to him. "I watched you girls and especially my Vee girl—"

Vee grinned.

"And I saw them learn to look for treasure in God and in others. I'm proud to be Vee's stepdad. Proud to know the S.A.V.E. Squad." He fished in his pocket and withdrew four tiny treasure chests. They lay in his broad palm, gold with red and blue trim.

The girls drew close and inspected them. "They are beads!" Aneta gasped, holding one up to the sun. "For our bracelets!"

A murmur ran through the backyard and then applause.

"To the S.A.V.E. Squad!" Dad said, raising his red plastic cup.

"Hey!" a new voice broke through the laughter and clapping. A tall, blond man with a deep tan wearing a Western shirt and jeans stepped through the wooden gate. "Did I hear S.A.V.E. Squad? I must be in the right place!"

"Uncle Dave!" Sunny shrieked and threw herself into the man's arms. Once he'd set her down, she turned and declared unnecessarily, "It's my uncle Dave Martin. You know, the one who's moving his horse place here!"

Dave greeted the rest of the Martin family and shook hands with everyone else. He protested he'd never remember everyone's name. When he got to Aneta's mom, she looked up at him laughing, and he laughed down at her. They were nearly the same height, so it wasn't far.

Vee poked Sunny. "Do you see what I see?"

Sunny poked Aneta. "Do you see that goofy look on my unmarried uncle's face? He likes your unmarried mom!"

Aneta poked Esther. "Do you see the funny look on my not-married mom's face? She looks like she wants to laugh and cry all at the same time. Why is that?"

The girls linked arms, and with Buzz in Vee's arms they moved to an empty corner of the yard.

Their very own Squad spot.

Lauraine Snelling is an award-winning author with more than sixty-five published titles, including two horse series for kids. With more than two million books in print, Lauraine still finds time to create great stories as she travels around the country to meet readers with her husband and their rescued basset, Sir Winston.

Kathleen Damp Wright teaches writing to Christian homeschoolers and can't wait to buy a student's first novel! When she's not dreaming up adventures for her characters, she's riding bikes with her husband, playing pickleball, and trying to convince her rescued border collie that Mom knows best.